Bossy

Interracial Romance Story Collection

Florian Green

Copyright © 2020 Florian Green

All rights reserved

Bossy is a work of fiction. The characters and events portrayed in this book are fictitious. Any similarity to real persons, living or dead, is coincidental and not intended by the author.

No part of this book may be reproduced, or stored in a retrieval system, or transmitted in any form or by any means, electronic, mechanical, photocopying, recording, or otherwise, without express written permission of the publisher.

ISBN-13: 9798692707352

Cover design by: Kelly Martin
Photography by: Tara Reed/The Reed Files
Library of Congress Control Number: 2018675309
Printed in the United States of America

Contents

Title Page	1
Copyright	2
Story Types	7
Paper	9
Flash Fiction Erotica: Butter	33
Soap	38
Oil	63
Flash Fiction Erotica: Milk	77
Teeth	82
Grateful Thanks	121

BMWW

Paper

Flash Fiction Erotica: Butter

Soap

BWWM

Oil

Flash Fiction Erotica: Milk

Teeth

Story Types

Paper - Contemporary Erotic Romance Novelette

Soap - Contemporary Erotic Romance Novelette

Oil - Erotic Short Story

Teeth - Slow-burn Adventure Romance Novelette

Paper

~United States, Present day~

Teddy bears were adorable. Soft, cuddly, safe; they were perfect for a comforting cuddle at the end of an exhausting day. Furry chests made soothing pillows. Charlotte had loved her teddy. His name was Sam. He'd always been there to reassure, console, praise, and counsel; she felt blessed by their relationship. It had been one of security, communication, and respect. The type so few women enjoy. He'd been a chubby bear though, and—despite gentle encouragement—his sporadic gym visits had never added firmness and definition to his frame.

Unlike the men she taught. Being a professor at St. Jacques, a top university, she presided over classes filled with specimens from generous gene pools. Women too, of course, but they didn't cause fluctuations of blood pressure like their male counterparts.

She would often stand in silent admiration at her podium, scanning along seat rows. So many of them; the gents were a sea of robust waves, rippling and shimmering, brimming with bounties below their vibrant surface. As a married professional however, she'd never planned underwater exploration. Even now, two years after her beloved Sam had passed on, she was still accepting the prospect of finding someone else. Their vows said they would part upon death, but he hadn't separated from her soul.

Still, it was pleasant to appreciate visuals at work. God, there were stunners. And St Jacques had such an international student body that she could enjoy a broad variety of masculine form. Strolling through campus was a woman's delight. She would pass towering Scandinavians with faces flawless and golden hair gorgeous; their broad shoulders and sinewy arms conjuring images of Viking warriors carrying off captives for ravishment. Slender caramel Arabs, with beards groomed to the finest follicle, would smile with hazelnut eyes singing of sunsets across sweeping sand dunes. Mild-mannered Asians made favourable impressions with their milk skin and spiked shocks of raven hair; t-shirts taut against wiry torsos.

But her favourite were the ebony hunks. Something about chiselled onyx made her panties and privates stick. And not just wetness below; delightful tingles of sin fizzed across her neck and scalp when she toyed with thoughts—fanciful, naturally—of what it would be like to give them a more bespoke form of education.

She was sitting in her office waiting on one such fellow. A 27-year-old master's student from Nigeria called Enofe Benjamin. There was one word to describe his looks: beautiful. Unfortunately for Enofe, his class results were not as impressive. He was doing a 1-year MRes with hopes of going on to a PhD, but progression was looking doubtful.

Leaning back with his grade paper in hand, she heard a familiar creak as the chair's back tipped to accommodate her shift in position. It needed changed. In fact, her whole office would benefit from a makeover. Or at least a spring clean and fresh coat of paint.

And an extra 20 square feet. The large desk she sat at took up half the room, and the rest was given to six chairs for tutorials. With smooth wooden arms and foamy blue fabric cushioning they were comfortable, but too bunched together. Students should be able to stretch legs and relax while flexing cerebrums, she thought. Especially with the enormous fees they paid.

Shelves behind her were crammed with academic works, including five ones she'd authored. Some people found economics a dry subject, but for her it represented one of the keys to true knowledge. It was a cliché, but money did make the world go round. That and other drives.

Eight years of staples, stationary, metal sleeve buttons and overzealous pen scribbles pressing through paper meant the surface of her chestnut brown desk had scuffs and scratches. Not that you could see much for all the essays, documents and books stacked and spread over it. Sturdy, the front and sides had panelling which stretched to within a couple of inches from the floor, concealing her lower half.

In recent months, she'd begun making use of that. There was a master's tutorial she had which was all-male. Occasionally, she would put on a skirt for teaching it. Then visit the department ladies' room five minutes before start time to remove panties and stockings. While the group would be busy discussing works of Hume and Marshall, she would slip off shoes and hike her lower clothing; supervising and nodding barefoot with legs spread wide, enjoying air against her womanhood. An inch of varnished oak shielding the delicate skin of her exposed sex from half a dozen rugged men. Charlotte had been a teddy bear's wife, but now she was starting to indulge in these little titillations. If nobody knew, where was the harm?

Today she had jeans on, but her bare soles were still enjoying freedom as she massaged them back and forth across the carpet's coarse fibres. She swept pencil shavings and eraser dust into her cupped hand and brushed them towards the wastepaper basket, smacking her palms together to clear the tiniest pieces. Acrid cedar mixed with vapours of cheap instant coffee rising from a lipstick-smudged mug, which was perched atop a stack of economics magazines.

Using the hem of her slim-fit cashmere cardigan, she rubbed smears from spectacle lenses. She often enjoyed a croissant and butter with her mid-morning cup. Unlike with Sam, the calories never settled, and her figure remained in healthy proportion.

Looking through the half-open sash window with its frame coated in cracked and peeling white paint, she saw the sun had made its usual appearance. Lush lawn was blanketed in golden beams. A lukewarm breeze was washing into her office, causing flutter and flap under paperweights. Contented warble drifted from beaks amongst branches of hickories lining the campus' cobbled streets.

A soft knock interrupted.

"Yes, come in."

The door opened and a handsome pair of sunglasses poked round. "Professor McCormack, may I please come in?"

What a polite guy. "Yes, of course. Please take a seat."

And in he came. What a babe. Not towering, but a decent height at about 5'10. She was 5'4 so most men seemed tall.

He placed a chair close to the desk. She could smell fragrance pulsing from his preened physique. Rose water and cinnamon mixed with leathery notes. Nose candy.

Placing his glasses on the desk, he sat. They were aviator style and framed in gleaming gold. Looked expensive.

His pigment contrasted with the frost-white shirt he wore. Short-sleeved, it revealed vascular arms. Biceps bulged and triceps twitched in perfect definition. There was no fat on his body.

Feeling flushed, she was rubbing her pale, pink-soled feet together under the desk. His strong hands looked like they could give a wonderful foot rub. She missed that.

Then she checked herself. This was serious. Slipping her shoes on, she sat forward holding the grade paper.

"So, your full name is Enofe Benjamin, just to clarify?"

"Yes, professor. That's correct."

"How have you been enjoying the Californian weather?" she asked with a reassuring smile.

He was perched, shoulders forward; their rounded peaks pressed tight against light cotton. "It's beautiful thanks, Professor McCormack. Things never seem quite so bad when the sun is shining, right?" he replied. His pronunciation was elegant, the tone gentle but with underlying firmness of masculinity.

"That's true. And please, you don't have to call me Professor McCormack. Charlotte is fine, really."

The smooth skin around his eyes crinkled as high cheekbones rose. His lips parted to reveal immaculate teeth. "Thanks so much, Charlotte."

"You're welcome. Now"—she gestured to the paper in her hands— "we have to discuss this situation, I'm afraid."

He sucked in air through perfect pearls. "Yes, I wish I could escape it, but we have to." Shuffling, he bit his lower lip.

Her natural tendency was to empathise with students. She'd had her own study struggles in years gone by. "Well don't get stressed out, ok? I'm here to help. We'll see what we can do."

"Thanks, pro—Charlotte. I hope you can help me."

"Ok so"—she re-analysed the data before returning to eye contact— "I'll just provide a little clarity on my role in all of this. Obviously, I didn't teach you during the MRes because of your module choices. But I am in charge of deciding who can progress to PhD. And that's whether they go straight from undergraduate, or—as in your case—from master's. I consult other staff, but the decision lies with me. If I sign off on it, you'll go through. So that's the good news ok?" She smiled again, hoping to calm his jitters.

"That's incredibly good news. Just tell me what I need to do, and I'll do it."

"Ok, well. Hold your horses. I think we need to talk about your grades. Your first essay in the macroeconomics module was an A plus, so that's fantastic. And then"—she scanned to confirm — "you got the same grade for your first econometrics essay. Also, great."

"Thanks. I worked really hard on them."

"I'm sure you did. It's no small thing to get those kind of marks. So well done, but…" she searched for gentle ways to express harsh facts. His powerful forearms were now resting on the desk. Spicy leather cologne was licking her nostrils.

"Erm, things haven't been easy. It's a long story."

"Would you feel comfortable sharing with me? I'm just trying to understand why you went from A plus to scraping C minus within a couple of months. I've talked to your lecturers and they said attendance has been very patchy. Can you help me understand what's going on?"

"Yes, ma'am. I'll do my best. And I think I'll be ok discussing things, as you seem so kind." His head was hanging, but he raised it to meet her eyes with a weak smile. What a sweetheart.

"Well, I appreciate having your confidence, Enofe. And I

think it's important I know what's going on. I have to evaluate the progress of each candidate before allowing them entry to PhD. And frankly"—she nodded at the grade paper— "with these results my tendency would be to recommend against attempting a doctorate. For example, you scraped a C minus for your dissertation. I would normally be expecting at least B plus at master's level if someone was going on to do a doctoral thesis. And that's for your benefit as well as ours. You don't want to spend four years of time and money only to fail at the end, I'm sure."

He was rubbing the tapered curls of his head and tapping the desk. "Yes, you're right. I think I have the ability though. It's just circumstances seem to be making it hard to study."

"Well, I think you have the ability too, so let's see if I can help with what's causing your grades to suffer?" she asked in a placating voice. Despite having no nephews, she'd become accustomed to an aunt's role on occasion.

"I'm always worrying about my family. There's so much political turmoil in Nigeria. My dad is the governor of Lagos State, and he has so many enemies. I would like to be there beside him. I want to help if I can. And my grandparents are in terrible health with cancer and I miss them. I also miss my sisters and feel they need my protection. Nigeria's not such a safe place for women, I'm sad to say. But my mum and dad wanted me to study here, to have a great chance for the future. They're spending all their savings on me. But what if I go back empty handed? It's so much pressure. I often feel sick with stress and anxiety.

"Oh dear. That does sound challen—"

"And my roommates party all the time. I say come on guys, what are you here for? Studying or partying? I can't sleep as they're always drinking and making noise."

"Oh no. They're also master's students?"

"Erm, yes."

"Which department? A colleague or I could talk to them? Politely, of course."

He hesitated, scratched his forehead and said, "Oh no, not possible. They're at another university. I met them through a website."

"Oh ok. Well when does your lease end? You could find another place to stay? Either alone, or with more mature roommates?"

He nodded. "Yes, I've been thinking of that. My lease ends next month so hopefully I can find another apartment. If I can get one for my budget. My parents are already stretched from the fees, to be honest, but it should be ok. I think my grades will improve dramatically if I can study in peace and sleep well."

"Yes, I think so too. I'm sorry to hear about all this. It must be tough."

"Thanks so much. I just want to make my parents proud, but I feel I'm letting them down." Liquid began forming around the rims of his lower eyelids as his voice pitched higher. "I'm so sorry, do you happen to have a tissue?"

She opened her desk drawer and brought out a tissue box. "There, it's ok," she said, reaching across and rubbing his hand. It was so smooth. "We'll work something out, ok?" It was against university protocol for staff to have physical contact with students, but she felt human touch was necessary sometimes. This poor guy was under such strain. She had a strong urge to hug him but rubbed his forearm instead. Warm stone passed under her palm as he dabbed at his reddened eyes.

"Leave it with me ok? I'll have a think about the best solution. But if I approve you, you'll need to make a solemn promise to work extremely hard, ok?"

He reclined, letting out a long sigh. His shirt's top two buttons were undone. Flexing pectoral peeked between the flaps. "Yes, ma'am."

"Ok, now try and relax today. I'll be in touch soon."

Unable to resist, she watched his bottom as he exited. Thin chino material revealed firm roundness. The cream colour and crease in the middle reminded her of apricots picked at her aunt's farm during childhood. Full of sweet natural flesh and juice.

It wasn't cool. She shouldn't be perving. But there was oh so much fruit at St Jacques. The place was an orchard.

∞∞∞

Growing tired of marking essays, Charlotte fancied another coffee but couldn't face more staff pantry granules. She locked her office and headed to the campus café.

After five minutes' walk in strong sunshine, she reached its shiny steel and glass front. The café was in fact a complex. Ground and basement floors held the coffee shop, while second and third were home to a burger bar and bistro, respectively.

A polite older gentlemen—most likely a fellow academic—was exiting and held the gleaming door open. Thanking him, she stepped inside and took off her brown tortoise shell sunglasses.

Vibrance pervaded in what was the hub for daytime socialising on campus. Staff and students congregated in throngs, and with good reason. Exorbitant tuition fees had financed cosy furnishings. Plush velvet and faux leather upholstery clothed chairs and booths. Wooden tables, floors and stairs were arrayed in sumptuous stain. The walls were encrusted with exposed stones to create rustic impression; plaster surrounding them was laid thick like buttercream. Air conditioning welcomed with wafts of coolness.

At the counter she ordered a small cappuccino, knowing it would be more than enough. Once, she'd ordered an extra-large and it was like a soup bowl. As if anyone needed that much caffeine.

Waiting for her drink, she surveyed for space beside the front windows. Nada. The entire floor was crammed. There would be an open spot in the basement, but she preferred gazing over sun-smooched greenery of grass and trees. Not hopeful of getting a decent seat, she made a last-minute request for her coffee in a takeaway cup. A shaded bench in the gardens would have to substitute.

She checked for liquid splashes before resting her cashmere-clad elbow on the counter. The place was bustling. Spoons clinked on china sounding silvery tinkles, packets were torn and tapped for sugary sprinkles; jaws clamped on paninis, smoothies were sucked, and croissants crunched, fingers tapped and swiped, foamy lips were flapped and wiped.

And the wonderful aromas. Charlotte hadn't been hungry but tantalizing smells were massaging her stomach to the point of surrender. Buttery vapours of pastry paraded themselves through the air, mingling with cheesy teases of quiche and luscious citrus scents of lemon loaf. She gave in and ordered a slice of cake. At size 8 it wasn't like she had to be super strict.

Her musings were interrupted. "Professor McCormack, how's it going?" The soft, lisping accent was familiar. She turned to be met with Alejandro, a Mexican student.

"Oh hi, Ale. Yes, not bad. Just treating myself to a carb injection. I assume you've been having skinny latte and wifi?" she asked in light-hearted teasing of his fitness lifestyle.

His olive-skinned cheeks dimpled and released a chuckle of admission. "Yes, professor, you guessed correct," he replied, brushing golden brown locks behind his ears. "I was wondering—"

"About your essay?"

"Yea. You know me, always worried."

"Well don't be. It was fine."

"Oh, you thought it was good?"

"You'll find out soon enough," she said with a polite but firm smile. "I'll see you in class on Friday, ok?"

"Ok, thanks, Professor. Have a lovely day."

As his V-shaped torso navigated to the door, she saw reaction ripple through girls seated at tables and booths nearby. Smiles, smirks and whispers; their eyes darting, gazing, yearning. He was a cute kid, to be sure.

But with emphasis on *kid*. He was 19. Her cut off—even in the darkest corner of fantasyland—was 21. If she couldn't enjoy banter over legal bourbon or beer, then it was borderline paedophilia. Muscles alone did not make a man.

Coffee and cake were bagged. Putting her sunglasses back on, she stepped out and left chatter and chirp behind.

∞∞∞

Landscaped grounds were a prominent feature of St Jacques' campus. The founder—and first president—had been a botanist and considered green spaces essential for aiding education through rest and relaxation. Tradition had stuck through the centuries and the university was now famed for its horticultural surroundings.

Charlotte headed towards a quiet section; her pink suede loafers crunching on golden gravel as she passed dozens of students enjoying casual outdoor culture on the lawns. They stretched like contented cats or sat cross-legged in circles trying to study while warm sun sapped academic resolve. There was even a shirtless douchebag under oak shade, serenading a couple of hippy chicks with sporadic guitar strums.

Walking down a mild incline, she pushed open a squeaking wrought iron gate to enter the gardens' most secluded part. A square-slabbed path wound past thick rose bushes; the petals of their pink badges quivering from the wind's tender kiss. Red-swathed maple branches high above formed a swaying canopy through which shards of sunlight oscillated from thin to thick, streaking across the ground with honey hues.

The route led to stone benches set inside a large semi-circular hedge, forming six separate alcoves. They faced onto a central rock garden with a range of cacti flourishing between smooth stone and jagged slate. Behind that was more hedging which separated the area from gardens beyond.

This place was called the Rock Garden, but it had gained the nickname of Teacher's Corner; leading students to assume—

incorrectly—that it was for staff. She was happy for the misunderstanding to continue. Easing into the closest booth, she welcomed shade given by tall clipped shrubbery. Pulling out her phone, she checked emails. New arrivals in her intranet account were mundane memos and moaning from fellow faculty. Nothing urgent.

Time for refreshment. She unfolded crinkly brown paper and popped the plastic cup top. Sipping through milky froth to reach the robust bitterness underneath, she let it flow over her tongue. Ah, that was better. And now for a munch on lemon loaf.

As she was fishing for food, a noise caused her to stop. Was that sobbing? She sat forward and peered into the next booth. Nobody. But there it was again. Definite crying. This time accompanied by a vehement nose blow. The high pitch of weeping told her it was a female. It seemed to be coming from the next bench over, but she couldn't see because of hedge which jutted to separate each alcove and give privacy. She wouldn't sit sipping and chewing while someone close by was upset. Taking the wad of café napkins, she walked to where the sound was coming from.

And was met by a former student. Kaitlyn? Kassie? Kendra? Her name was dancing about in Charlotte's memory bank. "Hey, you," she said in mild tone.

"Oh, hi"—she sniffed— "professor. I'm probably not supposed to be in here," she replied, beginning the shift to her feet.

Kendall! She waived her back down with a smile. "Don't be silly, Kendall. I just wondered if you were ok?" The answer was clear, regardless of reply.

"I'm ok, thanks for asking." Her light tan skin was blotchy crimson round her eye sockets. She was twitchy and holding a ragged tissue which was far past its absorbent capacity. Squeezed and sodden, moulded by her clasp; it looked like an emaciated apple core.

Charlotte offered her napkins. "You look like you could use these."

"Thanks so much." She peeled one and blew her nose into it hard. Then wrapped it in a ball and placed it on the bench. Then she took another and wiped her eyes, holding it in anticipation of re-use.

"Here"—she placed them into Kendall's lap— "Keep them. They always give too many. May I sit beside you?"

"Sure. And thanks a lot," she replied through sniffs.

She grabbed her coffee and cake and returned to perch beside Kendall.

Blonde, beautiful and athletic, she was also a brilliant student. She'd shone as an exemplary class member in the first year of her economics degree. No older than 20, she was one of these young people who inspires with their energy and zeal for life.

And now her face was a puffy picture of misery. Blue eyes bloodshot and brimming with fluid, she was holding back more tears. The sorrow was still being purged. What had upset her so much?

They stared at the sun-drenched rock garden. She presented the cake in its domed plastic container. "Want some? It's really good," she asked, peeling the clear cover from its opaque base.

Kendall looked at the large slice and gave a faint smile, replying, "Thanks, professor. But I don't think I can. Too sad."

She took a mouthful. The thick sponge was a delicate level of sweetness. But not satisfying. Funny how mood flavours food, she thought. "Too sad to enjoy cake. This has to be down to a guy."

Another weak smile broke. Followed by sniffling and nose clearing. "Yeah. A jerk."

"Ok. And would you like to tell me what happened with this jerk?"

"I don't know. I feel so stupid. That's why I came down here. My roomies warned me about him."

She took off her sunglasses and placed a hand on Kendall's shoulder. "Look at me, please." Teary eyes turned. "You are not stupid, ok?"

An "ok" was whimpered in reply. Her head hung low. The nose was blown yet again, sounding like a blocked trombone.

"Nobody, erm"—she took deliberate pause— "hurt you, did they?"

"No, nothing like that. He just suckered me with his lies. All he wanted was to sleep with me." And with that, the fluids flowed. She budged closer and rubbed Kendall's shoulder blade. Snivelling and spluttering continued for a couple of minutes before she calmed.

"This guy's at St Jacques?"

"Yeah. My roomies warned me, but I didn't want to listen. He's so hot, and he was so sweet to me; I thought I could change him. What is wrong with me?" The question was asked in anger.

"Nothing. It's called being human."

"Thanks, professor. I should have known better though. It wasn't just my roommates. A couple of girls in my classes told me stuff too. I should have listened."

"What kind of stuff?"

"Like he parties all the time in the clubs, drinking too much and chasing girls. Just wants to have a party every night. He has a penthouse at the marina. I've been there. It's really fancy."

"Marina? Wow. Pricey. But it sounds like he's going to fail whatever he's studying, with that attitude."

"He doesn't even care. He told me himself. He just wants to stay in the US long enough to get his Green Card and then citizenship. His family are rich and gave him a bunch of money, so he doesn't even need a degree. I think they kicked him over here to get rid of him, to be honest. He said he'd caused some trouble but wouldn't say what."

"So, how come a smart girl like you fell for this guy then? If people were warning you about him?"

"Same reason most other girls did, I guess. He's convincing. He said it was true he was a playboy but meeting me had changed that. He said he wanted to grow up and have a real relationship. Asshole."

"If its ok to ask, what was his excuse for not wanting to see you anymore?"

"He said his family won't accept me cause I'm not from their culture, so it would never work. But he doesn't even care what they think. He just got what he wanted and dumped me. I feel like shit. He used me."

She pursed her lips and gave Kendall's shoulder another rub. "I'm sorry. You're better off without that jerk anyway. And there are nice guys out there. Just takes time to find one."

"It's ok. I am done with men, believe me." She flicked her hands out towards the rocks in a gesture of riddance.

Resisting the urge to disagree—because she knew the vow would be broken—she offered calm consolation. "Ok. Its best you focus on school now." Her eyes had dried, and the twitchiness and sniffling had stopped. Talking had done her good. "You're going to be ok; I promise. Is this guy doing economics?"

"Yep."

"Is he in any of your tutorials? I can probably shift things around if he is, so you don't have to study beside him."

"Thanks so much, but he's not undergrad."

"Oh ok. I know it's being nosey, but do you mind if I ask his name?"

"Enofe."

∞∞∞

Charlotte was curled on the corner suite sofa in her living room. A large ball of orange fluff—like candy floss but with paws and face—was nestled in her lap. Every time her hand drifted from the squashy fur for more than a second, a grouchy request for attention would come out the front end. Tabitha, her Persian, was a real clinger. Now Sam was gone, she cuddled either cat or pillow of an evening. Often both.

Sipping on tart cherry and plum flavours, she stroked her companion and reflected on the day. Wasn't life bizarre sometimes? If just one seat had been free at the café's window area, she would never have spoken to Kendall. And heard the disturbing information about Enofe.

Was it all true though? Being an academic, she knew the

dangers of relying on a sole source to prove facts and reach a conclusion. Truth tended to be fumbled and fudged when nerves were in knots. And there was no doubt the girl had been upset. But there hadn't been an outpouring of anger. A couple of cuss words, sure, but it was heartbreak not hatred she'd seen. What was she to do?

Her feline friend, purring from petting, lifted her fluffy chin to be rubbed. She smiled and obliged. Tabitha—or Tabby, as she often shortened it to—was one of those breeds unfortunate to have a face which looked inherently miserable. The scowling expression reminded her of poor Kendall.

Charlotte had also been in that situation, a long time ago. The broken promises, the hollow feeling from being used and tossed aside had a searing sting; she swore she'd never suffer that again. Why did men never understand how deep those emotional daggers could plunge? Except Sam did. He'd got it. That was why she'd accepted his teddy physique. She'd traded sinew for sensitivity.

If handsome Mr Benjamin had been manipulating people—herself included—to achieve his own selfish ends, he was going to regret it. She wasn't a vindictive person, but men who ran rampant over women's emotions stirred loathing inside her.

Putting down her glass of merlot, she reached forward and lifted her phone from the glass-topped coffee table. This caused a meow of tuna-scented discontent. "Oh, stop moaning, you little grouch," said Charlotte in baby speak—she confessed to being one of those people—as she swiped the screen with one hand and rubbed thin silk ears with the other.

She'd settle the situation's truth for herself. And then act if necessary.
Opening her intranet mail, she wrote a message to Enofe Benjamin. It read like this:

Hi Enofe
I think I've come up with the perfect solution to your PhD progression. We should discuss it face to face though. I hope tomorrow's

suitable for you? I'll be busy all day, but if you come around 6:30pm I'll have time. I realise it's late, but I think you'll agree this is important.
Best wishes
Charlotte

It was around a minute later her phone pinged. The reply was short:

Dear Charlotte
That's great news! Thanks so much! I'll be there on the dot!
Thanks
Enofe

She had another mouthful of wine. Tabby was now stood with front legs extended on Charlotte's thigh; her planted paws giving a firm declaration of friendship. Revelling in caresses and massage from fingers around her neck and head, and humming with happiness like an organic motor, the face still displayed false depression. As she rubbed under grumpy girl's puffy cheeks, she broke into further baby talk, saying, "He shouldn't thank me just yet. No, he shouldn't, should he?"

∞∞∞

"Ok, that's me off. See you tomorrow. Happy marking," said Sarah the department secretary, buttoning her raincoat. She was usually last to leave.

"Ok, drive safely. I think there's going to be quite a downpour," replied Charlotte, lowering the roll blind. At 6pm, sunset was far from due, but charcoal clouds had brought evening early. She switched on the floor lamp. It lit the room's centre but kept the edge in shadows. Dim was desirable for this type of appointment.

Closing the door and sitting at her desk, she pulled out a

bottle of bourbon from the bottom drawer. It was used for occasional fortified coffee on frosty winter days. But today she needed tension tonic.

Its warmth spread down throat, through stomach and across limbs, soothing with internal canoodles. After another two large sips, stiff shoulder muscles began to ease as she reclined to familiar creaks; her mug of spirit cupped in both hands. Adrenaline had been building since late afternoon, and she'd found herself unable to focus on anything but what might happen with Enofe.

Placing the bourbon back in the drawer, she took hold of her compact pepper spray—small as a packet of chewing gum—and gave it a gentle shake to confirm full contents. It fitted inside her cardigan pocket. Just in case. She looked at her desk phone's interface. Campus security could be dialled with a one-digit tap. Unlikely that would be necessary, but it was reassuring to have them nearby.

She sipped. Grumbles echoed outside, escalating to booms. Waves of watery slaps battered glass while the sky's crying hammered on cobbles. Slivers of white light flashed through gaps between the blind and window frame, sending stripes of dazzle across her desk.

And then there was a knock. She drained the mug and set it next to a small mesh pot stuffed with slanted pens and pencils. It was time.

"Come in," she said over ongoing splash and bellow beyond the thin windowpane.

Enofe strode through the door, his stylish green raincoat shining from storm spatter. "Wow, it's a wild night." His face was energised.

"Isn't it just." Feeling internal prickles, she was glad of the whiskey shot kneading her nervous system. "Do you want to hang up your jacket?" She nodded at the coat stand.

"Oh, of course, otherwise I'll soak everything." He removed his jacket to reveal a peach polo shirt tight against his wiry body. The small woven symbol told her it was designer.

Placing one of the chairs close, he sat, fidgety and excited. "So, Charlotte, you have good news for me, or what?" he asked in a presumptive manner that gave pause.

"Yes, I think I do. Here"—she reached into the desk drawer and offered tissues— "for your face. Looks like you got drenched."

He plucked a couple of sheets from the box's papery plume. "You are so kind, thanks." He dried his handsome face and then lobbed the soaked tissues into the wastepaper basket as if shooting hoops. This guy was full of confidence. "So? Please don't keep me in suspense."

She leaned forward with a reassuring smile, catching notes of dry, woody lemon. Was that vetiver? "Ok, so. I've decided to let you progress to PhD. You'll be studying economics for another four years."

Leaning back, he said with a clap of hands, "Oh, that is wonderful news. Thank you so much. I can't tell you how relieved I am. I really—"

"Well hold on, because there's even better news," she said with cheeks bunched and nose wrinkled.

"Oh what? This is amazing. What news could be better?" he asked, sitting forward; mouth open in anticipation.

The wind was whistling, bombarding the rickety window with wet lashes. Another glimpse of nature's fireworks flashed beyond the blind; a thin glimmer zipping between them.

"Well, I was really touched by your words the other day. I'm in full agreement with you that worrying about your loved ones all the time is what's making your studies suffer. So"—she paused like a game show host about to reveal the star prize— "I've decided to make you a special case and let you do your doctorate via distance. From Nigeria. You'll be able to study *and* be with your beloved family. Isn't that wonderful?" she asked, ignoring his lips and focusing on answers from eyes.

His mouth closed. Then he began to stutter, "Well, I, I—"

"And I know, I know. It's not standard procedure, but don't worry. We'll organise plenty online resources and staff support for you. I want to make this work. You deserve to be back with your family." Her lips shiny with saccharin.

"But it might be better if I stay here, because—"

"It is what you want, isn't it?"

"Well, yes, but I think I also might be better staying here."

Case closed. She had no more empathy for him. Her tone grew stern. "Because you want to go out partying every night? And play games with pretty girls?"

"What?"—he drew his head back in unconvincing outrage—"Who on earth have you been talking to? I just think staying here would make my studies easier."

She pressed her teeth together, grating them. "Enofe, do you think I managed to become a professor at St Jacques by being an idiot?"

His tone lowered; the manner adjusted to appeasement. "No, of course not. I'm sorry Charlotte."

"Good, so—and it's now Professor McCormack to you—you don't think I'm a person of low intelligence, right?"

"No, Professor McCormack. Sorry if I—"

"But you continue to insult my intelligence."

"I'm sorry, I didn't mean—" Swagger was now stagger.

"You can stay at St Jacques and do your PhD here in the US."

"Oh?" His eyes peeled with refreshed hope.

"Yes, but not with your current attitude. Its not acceptable. You'll need to have behavioural adjustment education."

"Like in a clinic?" he asked with high pitch.

"No, like in this office. Right now."

"Oh, I see. It's just one session?"

"Yes. Do you agree?"

"And if I take behavioural adjustment, I can definitely stay here for my PhD?"

"That's the deal."

"Then ok. I agree."

"Good." She walked to the door and turned its circular lock switch, causing it to snap shut. Then, turning to face him, said, "Get undressed."

"Wha—why?" She sensed his surprise was at least half-genuine.

"Because this lesson will be done without your clothes on. Now go on"—she paused to look him up and down— "strip completely naked."

He stood and moved the chair. Facing her as she leaned on the door, his hands grasped the polo shirt's hem, hesitating.

"I haven't got all night. Now do you want to continue your studies or not?"

His answer was shown in action. He pulled off the polo shirt, revealing a masculine landscape of muscular peaks and plateaus. Brawny shoulders and biceps rippled at either side of diamond-cut pectorals and abdominals.

Holding the cool, hard brass of the doorknob with her palm, she ordered, "And the rest. Hurry up before I change my mind."

Slipping off his brown Chelsea boots—which were still speckled from the rain—he took off his socks and then fumbled at his belt. Kicking off the jeans, he placed them next to the rest of his clothes. And there he stood. In red and black striped silk boxers.

Wind howled and rain rasped. Another shimmer of light was followed by raucous complaint, as if the heavens had indigestion.

Charlotte was bathing in brazenness. She stepped forward and yanked the boxer shorts to his ankles. "Step out of them." Once he'd done so, she tossed them onto the pile of clothing and stood back, drinking in his shame. "Put your hands by your sides so I can see your cock."

"Professor McCormack, what is going on h—"

"Gone shy, have we? I thought you liked introducing that thing to women. Move your hands and shut your mouth."

Looking away from her, he did as he was told. Charlotte bit her lower lip and smirked. It was a thick one, hanging flaccid over bulging balls. 5 inches long by her estimate. She wondered how many hearts—and hymens—it had cracked.

Staring at his bare feet, he mumbled, "So what now?"

"Turn around so I can see your ass." The words popped in

rapid succession like projectiles.

He had the sculpted hind quarters of a thoroughbred. Thick muscle moulded in perfect plumpness. "Well, you're too big for me to put over my knee. You'd squash me"—she walked to the desk and patted its centre— "bend over here. Put your head down and stick your ass up fully."

"This is not professional."

"Well if you behaved better, you wouldn't need correction, would you? So, it's your fault. Now be quiet. I'm going to spank some decency into you."

The first slap's harsh report was partially drowned by raging sky. Her hand stung. "You're going to treat women with respect from now on. Is that clear?"

Grimacing from the impact, he said, "Yes, professor."

She swiped again, causing him to jolt. "I hear any more shit about you and your visa will be toast. Clear?"

"Yes, ma'am, very clear."

As a reinforcement, she smacked his ass as hard as she could, six times in succession; he sucked air through gritted teeth, the strapping buttocks fluttering from slaps. Her petit palm was blush, bristling with pins and needles. It was clear she could only do so much against the robust flesh of his buff backside. Looking at the gap between his thighs and the desk, she saw his flaccid cock had inflated. This boy was incorrigible.

"Stand up and face me." His vein-riddled shaft was pulsing proud. It had a bend in it; looked like an overripe banana. Breathing in short gasps, his tongue was red as raspberry. Moist with juice.

Panting, powerless, his eyes obedient; he stepped forward and cupped her small breast in a trembling squeeze, rubbing it between fingers and thumb through thin cardigan and bralette. Shockwaves of delight coursed in her chest. She hadn't been touched for over two years. But she wasn't going to tell him that.

"How dare you!" She took hold of his ear and drew their faces close. "Arrogant pig. Open your mouth. Stick out your tongue."

She enveloped it, sucking, then pressing, rubbing, the friction of their taste buds tantalising. Her toes tingling, knees trembling, their liquids mingling; forming glistening strings as she pulled back to catch gasps of air before plunging again between lips soft and luscious.

Holding his cheek in a firm pinch as the woody citrus of his scent pervaded, she scolded him. "You like using this to get what you want, eh?"

"Yes, I do."

"Well, I've got something for it to do." Fingers fumbling, she unzipped her jeans. Off they came. Then her panties. "I've got a job for that smart mouth."

She sat on the chair beside her desk. Spread. Cool air brushed bare thighs and feet. The command was direct: "Eat."

"What? Prof—"

"On your knees and eat!"

Enofe obeyed. Feasting, slurping, his thick tongue stretching and filling. The storm was still outside, but the true tempest raged between her legs. A flailing foot knocked over pencils and pens, sending them rattling across carpet. Clutching at his curls, she writhed, rocked, her crotch crackling. Fingernails dug into his scalp as torrential rain battered, saliva drenched, and juices spattered.

"Get that tongue right into my pussy. As deep as it'll go." Mouth in a soft clamp over her sex, only his eyes nodded as he ate in obedience, pushing further in. "Good, very good. Now lick my clit. Flick it with your tongue. Ah, that's it. Good boy. Lick, flick. Don't you dare stop"—she pressed his sticky face against her dripping lips— "lick it harder. Lick it harder. I said lick!"

Thunder cracked like a shotgun. "I'm gonna, I'm gonna," she squealed. The feeling was so exquisite no pitch could reach high enough. Hands clamped around his skull; her knees constricted, holding his face in place. And then her scream unleashed, lost in the harsh flare and bang of Thor's hissy fits.

Cleansed of sexual tension, her feeling was one of utter relief. Patting his head, she panted a simple, "That was nice."

Stickiness coating his lips and chin, he stood in naked glory. A sexual champion. Subjugated.

She pulled on her panties and trousers, zipping them shut, then stepped into her loafers. Grabbing his grade paper from her desk, she thrust it into his chest, saying, "Wipe your mouth with this."

Holding the crinkled page, he tried to make an offer. "Can we—"

"No, we can't. Get dressed and get out."

"But I thought we could—"

Looking at his crescent erection with its fat, swollen head, she tutted and said, "I've got what I needed. Go home and finish yourself off. Now get dressed and get out. I won't ask you again."

∞∞∞

Two weeks later, Charlotte was sat in a booth by the campus café's windows, enjoying sunshine and smoothie. She'd honoured the deal and allowed Enofe to do his PhD. With his current level of commitment, he'd give the university 200,000 dollars in fees and fail anyway, which was fine. Smirking between straw sucks, she recalled how dejected he'd looked leaving her office. It had been made clear to him that mentioning their stormy interaction to others would see his US party time curtailed with immediate effect.

She dabbed her mouth with a napkin and tossed it aside. The path was bustling with happy young people, milling in golden warmth. There were so many couples among the student fraternity. Hands, arms, even the occasional pinkies were linked and held in sweet announcements of affection.

It was time for her to find a new teddy bear. Not a replacement—as that wasn't possible—but someone to give her the love and affection she needed. Sam would understand. He'd always made her happiness top priority. But was there anyone out there that could even come close?

"Professor!"

"Kendall. Nice to see you, and hi Ale. How are you guys doing?"

"Great, we were just deciding what to do this weekend," replied Kendall. Her slender arm was tightly wrapped around Alejandro's shredded bicep. She was glowing.

"Oh, that's lovely. Well I hope you guys have a wonderful time."

"Thanks, professor. Have a great weekend," said Alejandro, opening the door for Kendall; her bright shining eyes infused with joy.

"Thanks. And you two behave yourselves, ok?"

Kendall, besotted with her hunky Latino, nodded and smiled, saying, "You're the boss."

Off they went, her leaning in tight at his side; him protectively cutting a path through the crowd, carrying her bag. It was a beautiful thing.

Yes, she thought, I am the boss.

Flash Fiction Erotica: Butter

~Bermuda, Present day~

Brooke was wrestling with emotions. Days like this—the type all ladies had—saw swings between rapid irritation and intense craving for fornication. The latter surging faster now she was back at home, away from niggling workplace toxicities.

She'd been seething in secret all day in the office. Little annoyances—that she usually dismissed—had grown wings. But they hadn't flown away. Instead, co-workers' incessant chattering and jabbering had pecked at her skull like a flock of minimum wage woodpeckers; their goal to either floor her with a migraine or have kindly men in white uniforms escort her to a waiting ambulance.

Slipping on a pink cotton nightdress and clean panties—the ones she'd had on all day were sticky—she curled on the sofa. Soft suede felt smooth under soles and calves as she massaged them against the cushions.

Thank God tomorrow was Saturday. She'd be able to catch up on sleep then immerse herself in the pages of another glorious romance novel; the elegant words would tranquilize turbulence of soul. If only more time could be given to such literary heaven.

Right now, though, she craved divinity in different measure: A man. She needed cock. Preferably one with length and girth. Pushed deep into a taboo passage. The thought of it had her chewing lip, grating teeth and tapping on Kindlr profiles far lower than her usual standards. Fuck it, this was an emergency.

But then a random guy from Kindlr would have to wear a condom. Because she was horny, not crazy. And anal just wasn't the same with a rubber. She liked to feel the hot, gooey cum dripping out her asshole. What was she to do?

The room was humid. Maybe cooling up top would reduce the furnace below? Listening to the air conditioner bleep open its wafting flaps, she walked across polished kitchen tiles for an ice-cold cola. The bottlecap tinkled; she swigged, stretching like a feline while feeling internal washes of chilled bubbling soda.

Better. But she still wanted to get fucked in the ass. Her toy was broken; maybe she could finger herself and pretend it was a cock? A quick check in her bedside drawer confirmed there was no lube left. Squeezed flat and rolled to the hilt; not even the tiniest dollop was gleanable from the blue and white tube. What would substitute?

The doorbell chimed. Peering through the peephole, she saw it was the new guy from two doors down. She'd heard Elsa the old woman next door mention his name. Jack? John? Jimmy?

"Hey, I'm Jake. I'm really sorry to bother you. I just wanted to introduce myself to all the neighbours. I would have done it sooner, but I've been busy at the clinic." She listened, but not through lips; his chestnut eyes were striking, magnetic even.

Broad-shouldered, about 6 feet tall with jet black hair and stubble the same colour, his shoulders and arms were thick, taut against blue cotton. No wedding ring. Looked early thirties. Prime meat.

"I'm Brooke. Nice to meet you, Jake"—she motioned to the cola—"would you like to come in for a cold drink?"

"Oh, thank you so much. Sounds great."

She patted the sofa arm. "Make yourself at home."

Opening the fridge, she reached for another cola, and saw the yellow tub of spreadable butter. She placed it on the kitchen counter.

"Would you like a sandwich, Jake?" She handed him the bottle, hoping he didn't see her hand trembling.

"Oh, no thank you. That's so kind of you though."

Walking in front of him, she stood with hands on hips. "What about an ass sandwich?"

He drew the bottle's mouth from his own, eyes flaring wide.

"Erm, excuse"—he stammered— "excuse me?"

"Are you married? Girlfriend?"

He took another glug. "No, I'm single."

"May I be direct?"

"Well"—he shook his head with a nervous laugh— "I think you already are."

Smiling, she said, "You said you work in a clinic? Are you a doctor?"

"No, I'm a dentist."

"Good enough." She leaned forward so his raven bristles were almost tickling her nose. Crisp citrus cologne was pulsing from masculine pores. "Because"—she turned away from him— "I need a medical opinion. Do you mind?"

"Well, I suppose not. I—"

"Do you think this is a healthy ass?" She lifted her nightdress waist high. Craning to see his reaction, she saw his mouth was half-open as he stared at her flimsy bikini-cut panties. She knew damn well that men drooled over her voluptuous pink derriere.

His breathing was starting to grow rapid. Shuffling forward, he perched on the sofa cushion. "It's very healthy, yes."

"Oh, but what am I thinking? You can't give a proper evaluation over clothing. It's better I'm bare bottomed." Holding her nightdress rolled under her armpits, she slipped her panties down, kicking them into the living room corner. "There. Now you can examine better. What do you think?"

Growing huskier in tone, he said, "It looks like a juicy peach."

"What's your opinion about anal sex?"

She could hear his voice shaking. "I think it's fine."

"And what about using butter as lubricant?"

"Also fine."

"And condoms?"

"I'm clean."

"Sure?"

"Yes. I had a check-up 2 weeks ago. Do you need the—"

She pulled the nightdress over her head, leaving her naked

in front of bulging eyes. "Get the butter. Rub it on your cock. I want to be fucked in the ass."

Dropping his jeans and boxers with scrabbling fingers, he smeared thick butter up and down his thick black cock. It was a good length too; about 8 inches in its already erect state. A firm challenge she was ready to accept.

"Where do you want me?"

"Over the kitchen table."

She lay her head on its side and pushed her hips up, spreading cheeks. Hungry for an ass fucking. Ravenous. "Jake"

"Yes?"

"Please go slow, ok?"

"Don't worry, Brooke." He pushed a buttery finger up her bottom. She licked her lips, savouring the delightful sensations, oozing a soft moan. "Is that ok?"

"Yes"—she rubbed her palms up and down the smooth, varnished tabletop— "you're very gentle. It's so good. Now put your cock up."

He took hold of her hips in a firm clasp and nestled his tip against her asshole. She could feel it teasing the tight skin folds of her puckered hole. And up the cock started to slide. Gasping—despite his gentleness—she clasped the table edges, taking deep breaths, accepting him into her most shameful place. So delicious. Overwhelming.

He shuffled forward as his greasy dick eased up, stretching the skin with tender pressure. It had been a while, but the delights of anal sex were all brought gushing back.

His entire erect length was up her back passage. And then the soft, measured pumping began. This guy knew what he was doing. Fabulous jolts of pleasure tingled and zapped as his crotch slapped against her quivering rosy cheeks. He fucked in delicate humps, their bodies bumping, colliding in velvety touch, her soft skin against his hairy crotch. Furry balls padded against her pussy with rhythmic knocks; her knees trembled, she grunted as the creaking table shunted, wood squeaking, Brooke squealing, "So good! So fucking good!"

Tempo quickening, the battering became more robust; thrusts, stabs, deep inside her bottom; knees quaked, wood rattled, as he rasped, "I'm sorry, I'm gonna have to cum. Your asshole's just too tight." His voice was desperate, trying to cling on.

Letting out a shout, he gripped hard and spasmed into her ass. Groaning, grinding, his semen squirted up her passage hot and thick; only to drip back down onto the tiles as he withdrew his spent cock, panting.

"Wow. That was incredible. Thanks for welcoming me to the neighbourhood!"

"Thank you. That really cleared my head"—Brooke gave him a kiss on his sweet lips—"you don't know how much I needed that."

Soap

~United Kingdom, Present day~

Janice picked up her phone yet again. Yawning, she checked messages. Nothing new. No funny videos, no memes, not even a hello from one of her sisters. Nothing.

It had only been ten minutes since she last looked, but still, why was nobody speaking? She sighed. The lockdown had been in effect for six weeks. All the disruption was starting to overwhelm.

Slipping the phone into her pyjama trouser pocket, she walked to the kitchen and opened the fridge's freezer compartment. Sliding out the top drawer halfway, she looked at the litre of ice cream nestled between bags of frozen vegetables and cardboard packets of processed chicken and fish. It was strawberry cheesecake, her favourite. That was why it was two scoops from empty, even though she'd only bought it the morning before.

When she'd been in the supermarket, staring at it on its shelf, her resolve had been firm: Don't buy it. Not for people on diets.

Then she'd made a promise it would be rationed out in scoops of two after each dinner, as an evening treat. Everything was healthy, in moderation. That was the deal.

And it had been broken the same day—of course—with a binge on both dairy and drama in front of the TV. Looking at the belly bulging under her nightclothes, she pushed the drawer back in, cursed her feeble attempts at self-discipline, and closed the freezer. No snacks. Dinner was only a few hours away.

Turning around to the worktop, her eyes were met by three bottles of South African red. They'd also found their way into the shopping trolley, against any form of sensible judgement.

Just one glass? But would she be able to stick to that? The last time she'd said similar, one afternoon tipple had become two bottles. The evening had been a blur, and the following morning spent with her head hovering above the toilet bowl. Lockdown was eroding her usual standards of moderation. She opened the cupboard above the microwave and stashed the wine inside. Out of sight, out of mouth.

A shower would make her feel better. Having not washed or changed in four days, her armpits told her the time was ripe and so was she. Under normal circumstances, when the primary school she worked at was open, she would have been clean, groomed, and in a different outfit daily. Janice took pride in her appearance and wanted to be a healthy role model for the children she taught, which was why her expanding waistline over the last few years had become a source of distress. It was never a good thing to be unhealthy, but, at 51 years old, every excess pound on her frame was unnecessary weight and risk being carried. Why did all the sinful things have to be so tasty?

She went to the bathroom and locked the door. But why bother? The divorce had been finalized over ten years ago, and no other men visited except her sisters' husbands when everybody came round for dinner. She unlocked the door and opened it wide. There was nobody to see her undressing, and steam would clear quicker.

She laid out a plastic mat on the bathtub floor, ensuring all suction points were attached to the ceramic. Then a heavy cloth mat was spread on the tiles. The whole room was prone to getting slippery and she'd almost taken a tumble twice before. Now floor coverings were always secured before turning on the showerhead.

Her pink floral pattern pyjamas were looking a bit grubby.

She unbuttoned the top and dropped it in the laundry basket. Unlike her two less developed sisters, she was wearing a bra during the lockdown. The strain on her back was just too much without the reinforced support. Plus, despite their size, they performed well against gravity, and she'd been told bras kept them that way. As she unhooked and opened it from the front, her pale freckled boobs sprang out, as if they relished the freedom. Trousers and panties were next in the basket. They were both size 14. She suspected a 16 would feel more comfortable around her waist but could never bear to take larger ones off the rail when browsing in shops. She kept telling herself dieting would prevail and buying bigger clothes would prove to be a waste of money.

The shower's spray was hot against her skin, soothing. Opening one of the gels on the shelf, she squeezed a generous blob of the thick soapy liquid into her palm. Its silky texture oozed between her fingers, as she worked a lather on her body. It had coconut and pineapple aroma, which reminded her of happier days; pina coladas by the pool in Tenerife.

Special attention was given to her crotch, as it was covered in a triangle of thick blonde pubic hair. She'd stopped shaving years ago. It seemed a waste of time when the only person to touch there was herself. Besides, using soap and hot water was just as hygienic as keeping it bald. The sides got a trimming every few weeks, but that was it. Butterscotch in colour and soft under her fingertips, she enjoyed massaging the gel into her mound. This bush had grown on her.

As usual, she made sure to lift her breasts one by one and wash everywhere, including underneath. Rinsing was also important, as soap residue caused her itchiness. What a chore making sure these things were clean. If she'd been braver, she might have considered a reduction. The thought of lying on an operating table was too scary though, and she'd learned to accept the burden.

The shower done, she dried herself with a towel and started to wrap it around her upper body. But again, why bother? The blinds on her bedroom window were closed anyway. She strode across the carpeted hallway and began fishing clean underwear out of her dresser. Over that went jogging bottoms, a t-shirt, and a thin sweater.

Once clothed, she pulled the blinds to welcome warm rays. The young couple next door were returning from their daily walk. Everyone was allowed 1 hour of outdoor exercise a day, and motivated people—like her neighbours—seemed to make effective use of it. They must have been in their mid-20s. Such a lovely match. She'd chatted to them a few times over the garden wall, and they were always laughing and smiling. Good-looking and slim, they had more than ice cream and vino to provide comfort of an evening. As they entered their front door, the girl's high-pitched chattering and giggles were a song of satisfaction and happiness.

Was she envious of the things they were getting up to? The answer wasn't certain. She'd almost forgotten what it was like to enjoy bedtime with a man. It had been ten years, and she was now used to being alone. In non-lockdown Britain, even her fingers were seldom used. She had a job, family events, and spa membership that kept her busy.

However, this surreal and lonely situation, which involved being stuck indoors most of the time, and unable to burn off energy doing laps in the pool, had caused her manicured digits to creep inside her panties increasingly. It was every morning now she found herself looking to get lost in the labyrinth of pleasure.

There were still two episodes left of the Last King to watch, so that would kill a couple of hours. Then she would make Thai green curry for dinner, with salad on the side, not rice, and have one glass of wine with it. One glass, and only because it was Friday, despite every day feeling the same in lockdown.

Back in the living room, she switched on the 42-inch TV, planting herself lengthways amongst the cushions of the sofa. Her bare soles were soothed by licks of cool leather. While flicking through the channels with the remote, she grabbed her phone. The lock screen was showing a notification type she didn't recognize. Swiping on it to expand the information, she was surprised to see it was from her Scouting for Couches app. She'd received a request to stay at her home for 3 nights, from an Aaron Clarke. How curious. Putting the TV on mute, she unlocked her phone to investigate further.

Scouting for Couches was like a homestay company, except it wasn't paid. Travelers—mostly young people—would request accommodation at hosts' homes for the purposes of cultural exchange, socializing, and networking. And it helped people with limited budgets reduce their accommodation costs. Members had profiles with pictures, a detailed biography, and references from other users who had met or stayed with them.

Janice was a premium host, meaning she'd paid 75 pounds for a lifetime membership. She had only ever accepted females—for security reasons—and even then, just half a dozen guests had asked to stay over the 5 years she'd been active. Leicester wasn't a tourist hotspot. It must have been around 18 months since she last had a backpacker from Scouting for Couches. That had been an intrepid young woman from Norway who was undertaking the colossal walk from Land's End to John O' Groats. Hilde had needed a place to rest while her route led through the Midlands. She remembered wishing for that kind of raw determination in her own life.

She opened the app to see what Aaron Clarke had to say for himself.

∞∞∞

His was the sole message in her Scouting for Couches inbox. It read like this:

Dear Madam Worthington
I know this isn't the most opportune time to be requesting a stay at your home, but due to the lockdown here in England, as well as the lockdowns across the globe, I've found myself unable to return home from my travels in your beautiful country.
Last week I bought a ticket to my country of Barbados, but it was suddenly cancelled without explanation two days later, and I haven't yet received the refund. This has left me short on money and I'm struggling to find suitable accommodation while I try to get in touch with the airline to sort it all out.
I know I've requested 3 nights, but if you're able to even host me for 1 single night it would be a massive help and I would be forever grateful. And looking at your profile, I know that you prefer to host female guests, but I'm hoping you can make an exception in my case. I've tried asking male hosts, but nobody has replied yet.
Best wishes and God bless you
Aaron Clarke
P.s. I saw in your profile that you're a teacher. I'm also hoping to be a teacher one day.

The message gave a good impression, and she felt bad for him as a young man stranded so far from home. Her inclination was to reject his request though, as in the past she'd always been unsure of hosting men. On top of that, the lockdown wasn't being implemented for fun. Coronavirus, although past its peak, was still killing between 500-700 people a day. For all she knew, he was infected. And she wasn't elderly but was far from a youth. Being overweight was a significant risk factor too, so she had been reading. Covid-19 didn't terrify her, but she didn't fancy following in the Prime Minister's footsteps. It had sent him—a younger man than her—to ICU and almost ended him.

Having said all that, Janice had nothing but time, so she decided to click on his profile for a nosey anyway. He was a premium guest member, which required the submission of credit card details,
so that went a small way in reassuring her of his legitimacy. A significant percentage of users on the app tended to have limited, free accounts which could be signed up to with any name and discarded without a trace. Once you paid you had a measure of accountability. So that was a plus for Aaron.

23 years old and from Bridgetown in Barbados, he was studying a B.Ed. in primary education. She was pleased to see a man taking an interest in what was such a female-dominated field. He also had an impressive 57 references from other hosts. Clicking on the list, and filtering them for 'do not recommend', she saw there were no negative comments. Quite the opposite. Scrolling, she saw enthusiastic recommendations about his conduct and cleanliness. At least every third person or so singing praises of his behaviour and committal to house rules was female.

It appeared he was a decent young man then. She clicked on his photos. He had just one, which must have been taken at a family celebration. He was standing alongside a man and woman around Janice's age and a group of other younger people. All were wearing smiles, as well as long, loose-fitting garments with ornate necklines and sleeves. The shoulders were broad. And he looked tall, at least compared to the woman she assumed was his mother. Handsome boy.

So, she concluded, in terms of safety, in a normal situation, he would have been ok to stay. But this was lockdown Britain. What if he brought Covid-19 into her semi-detached? No, it had to be a no. Her thumb gravitated to the decline button. She hesitated. Where would this boy sleep if he was unable to find a safe place? They could talk over the phone and discuss the steps he had taken to protect himself from the virus? If she didn't feel comfortable, she would reject his request. Against her inner voice of reason, she

tapped maybe instead.
She wrote him a reply:

Dear Aaron
Thank you for your nice message. I'm so sorry to hear about your unfortunate situation. You're right that I wouldn't normally host a male guest, but looking at your profile and references, and the fact you're stranded so far from home due to this terrible pandemic, I feel I may be able to make an exception. However, before I confirm your stay, I would like to talk to you on the phone or via internet call.
Please contact me via any of the below methods:
Phone – 06678654399
Messenger – Jworthington12789
Close Up – janice@leceisterschools.gov
If you have any difficulties with those, then please give me your number and I'll call you.
Best wishes
Janice

Around 5 minutes later her phone began to vibrate. It was a messenger audio call from a new number. She tapped the answer button and put it on speaker.
"Hello?"
"Hello, is that Madam Worthington?"
"Yes, is this Aaron?"
"Yes, madam, this is Aaron Clarke. So nice to meet you."
How adorable that he'd clarified his surname. As if she sat around waiting for calls from men named Aaron on a regular basis. "Hi Aaron. May I ask where you are now?"
"Of course, I'm currently in a supermarket. The name is Freshco. The lady at the counter was so kind as to give me the wifi password."
His voice was gentle and melodic. He spoke in a quasi-antiquated fashion she found charming.

"Oh, I see. And do you know which Freshco it is?"

"I'm not entirely sure, but I think it's Glenfield. The last sign I saw before I found it was Glenfield."

"Oh yes, I know it. It's not too far from here. I'd like to ask you one or two questions if that's ok?"

"Yes, Madam Worthington, I'm at your disposal. Please fire away."

"I suppose what worries me about having you stay is the Covid risk. You haven't been showing any symptoms, have you? Like temperature or cough, things like that?"

"No, I really am as healthy as a horse. And I don't think horses can catch it."

He was cute. "Well, ok, that's good to know. But I will say if you turn up and I think you look sick then I won't be able to allow you into the house. I hope you understand that."

"Oh, I completely understand your situation. It's kind of you just to even consider me as a guest during this challenging time. Believe me, in any case, there will be no malice towards you if I can't stay."

His tone was calm, sincere. He seemed like a gracious person. "And have you been social distancing?"

"Absolutely, Madam Worthington. I'm careful about social distancing. If I kept my distance from people in Leicester any further, I'd be in Ireland at this moment."

She laughed out loud. Humour given in his Caribbean accent was quite lovely. "Ok, that's good. And have you been washing your hands properly? And please call me Janice. You're making me feel old with all this formality."

"Oh, thank you so much, Janice. Well, I haven't been able to wash with soap so many times, but I have a big bottle of sanitizer which I use about ten times a day. But I'm really looking forward to a hot shower soon. I hope you can help me."

"I see. That's ok –"

"The only thing that concerns me is what may have collected on my clothes, as I haven't been able to launder them for a few days. If you decide you can accommodate me, I'll put all my unclean clothes in the laundry upon arrival. If that's not offensive to you."

"No, that wouldn't be offensive. It's very thoughtful of you, actually."

"I'll be honest with you, Janice, last night I slept in a park and it was a bit uncomfortable."

"Oh my. That can be dangerous! Are you ok?"

"It was more the chilly air and hard ground that were tough. Believe me, the parks we have in Barbados are far more dangerous. There's usually somebody roaming around to rob you."

She gave a half-laugh but also felt bad at hearing this nice guy had been forced to sleep rough. Deciding to conquer her Covid fear and show a Samaritan attitude, she agreed to host Aaron. A tsunami of gratitude smacked her ears. Wave after wave. What an adorable boy.

After they'd finished talking, she opened the Scouting for Couches app and pressed the accept button, then sent her full address and directions.

She decided to cook enough chicken curry for two people, hoping he liked Thai food. She chose a strong Syrah from amongst the three reds in the cupboard and cracked it open. A rich bouquet of jammy, peppery vapours was released as it splashed inside the large glass, which she filled around three-quarters full.

By the time the doorbell rang two hours later, she'd finished the bottle and was halfway through a second one.

∞∞∞

Upon hearing the chime of the bell, Janice muted the TV and

plonked her empty wine glass on the wooden coffee table. It skidded along the varnished surface on its base, and almost fell off the other side. She lurched from the sofa and staggered forward, losing her balance for a second. She would have to buy wine with a lower alcohol content next time. Looking in the mirror above the mantelpiece, she could see grapes had infused their colour into her cheeks. Things were fuzzy, but her hangover would be manageable if she swapped wine for water.

She teetered to the front door and opened it to be met by Aaron standing on her garden path. His smile was broad, showing off his impeccable dental hygiene, as he said, "Janice! It's so good to meet you in person! See? I'm social distancing until I receive your permission to enter."

"Hello Aaron, yes it's nice to meet you, and that's also very considerate of you," she garbled. Conscious she would appear unsteady on her feet; she held the door frame. "Did you have trouble finding a bus? I didn't think it would take you so long." Porch tiles felt cold against uncovered toes, and evening breeze caused shiver through thin sweater.

"I'm so sorry for arriving at night. I waited around for the bus, but it didn't come. I decided to walk it. But that's ok, it's all good exercise. So, do I look healthy enough to be your guest?"

Keeping a grip on the wooden frame, she leaned forward. He looked fine. No cough, eyes seemed normal. He was sporting a light beard that suited the contours of his face. His hair was shaved quite high at the sides, and the top was a black spiky sponge of thick curls. Far more rugged than in the photo. At about six feet tall, he was much taller than her. "Yes, I think you'll be fine. But please remember to cough or sneeze into—"

"Like this?" Where his forearm joined his upper arm was covering his face. "My dad's a doctor, and taught me that many years ago," he said smiling.

"Exactly. Ok, would you like to come in?" She stood to the

side, bumping her back on the corridor wall, and gesturing with her arm into the hallway.

"Well, I really am not wanting to bring anything into your home which might be on my clothes, so if it's ok I will put them in a bag if you have one?" He pulled off the straps of his rucksack and placed it onto polished porch tiling.

"Oh yes, the clothes in your backpack. They can go in the laundry. I'd forgotten about that."

As she swayed towards the kitchen to find a bin bag, she heard him call, "May I lock the outer door?"

"Yes, please. It's self-locking. Just close it," she shouted out the side of her mouth while fishing around under the sink. Why were things always more difficult to find after drinks?

When Janice arrived back at the porch, she was met with quite a sight. He was standing there in his underpants. All the clothing he'd had on sat in a big pile on the floor.

She was glad her cheeks were already flushed from wine. What a body! He looked like he'd been carved from black marble. Rippling with sinew, every muscle on his physique was visible, vascular. And the biceps, oh my. They must have been about 18 inches, all honed masculine flesh. She'd been to the National Museum in Greece before, and it was like their statue of Zeus was stood in her porch.

"As I said on the phone, I hope it's not offensive to you, but it's best to just put everything in the laundry without taking it through the house. I hope it's ok to wash my bag too, as it may have encountered the virus."

Realizing she had been staring too long, she placed the bin-bag next to the clothes, and said, trying to sound unphased, "Ok if you just want to put all of it in there, I'll be sure to wash it and get it all in the dryer. I have plain black pyjamas I can give you for now. They're just t-shirt and trousers, not feminine looking. Is that ok?"

"You're so kind," said Aaron as he finished stuffing his things into the bin bag. Janice looked at his black and white striped briefs. They were the type with the broad white elastic around the top, where the designer's name was written in large bold. She could see the pouch had a considerable bulge. Looked like he was hiding a pair of thick socks in there.

"Shall I put my undergarments in the bag too?"

Alcohol sometimes made her say and do unpredictable things. And this was one of these times. She surprised even herself when the words came out. "Yes, I think so. Slip your underpants off." Where on earth had that come from? Was it the wine? Or had 6 weeks of lockdown loneliness affected her sense of decency?

Hooking his fingers into the waistband, he hesitated and gave a shy smile. She got the feeling he hadn't expected her to say yes.

Her breath quickened in anticipation of the secret soon to be revealed. She hoped he wouldn't notice her voice shaking when she said with a dismissive tut, "I'm 51 years old, Aaron. You've got nothing I haven't seen before."

When his underwear came down, she realized how wrong that assumption was. Out flopped a gigantic penis. It was as thick as bratwurst and about 8 inches long even while soft. Below it in his sack hung two testicles the size of boiled eggs. Everything was trimmed and neat. She hadn't seen a nude man in a decade, and never one like him. Her undies were getting damp.

He'd moved his hands to cover up, but they weren't able to conceal his length. She smiled, and said in slurred reassurance, "You really have nothing to be ashamed of. I'm old enough to be your mum. Now let's get you up and into the shower, shall we?"

With his pants in the bag, she made a loose knot in the top of it and dropped it in the corner of the porch. "I'll deal with that once we've got you in the shower. The bathroom is at the top of the stairs. Up you scoot now; there's a good lad. I'll come in and make sure you're all set."

"Uh, yes. Thank you." He made his way past, completely naked. Following behind him on the stairs, she fixed her eyes on his bare bottom. The taut, supple skin shifted with each step, from side to side. Rounded with muscle and flesh, it was like a juicy chocolate peach. As with the rest of him, his buttocks were Olympian. The wonders of male nudity had been forgotten so long, but his beautiful body being exposed in its entirety was causing a rapid reawakening.

Walking into the bathroom, he asked, "May I use one of your towels, please?"

"Yes, you may. But first, please stand over by the sink while I lay these mats. I don't want you slipping and hurting yourself." She was turning all bossy on this young man, and he didn't seem to object.

Obeying, he sidled past, with his granite-like pectorals brushing against her breasts. She caught a hint of his scent. Salt and vigour.

She placed the two mats and switched on the shower. "They'll stop you slipping."

"Thank you, Janice, I—"

"Because things will get wet, with you in here," she said into his eyes. Plain shameful. Wickedness was stirring, and she found herself embracing it.

With a nervous swallow, he looked away, saying with a tremble in his voice, "You're so caring. May I get in the shower?"

"Yes, you may." She felt her heart flutter as his ripped physique squeezed past her again, the giant cock swinging as he stepped into the tub.

He stood perusing the collection of gels and shampoos on the shelf underneath the shower and chose the coconut and pineapple one she had used earlier. He flipped its plastic lid and sniffed at the hole.

"That's nice stuff. I used it earlier." Trying to sound casual and not betray her enjoyment of his nakedness, she asked, "Maybe I should help you wash your back? You can't reach it to scrub it properly, and we do want to make sure you're fully disinfected, don't we?"

He gave an embarrassed grin and said, "Are you sure it's not too much trouble? I don't want to be a burden to you."

"It's no trouble at all. Making sure you're clean keeps us both safe, doesn't it? And you did sleep on the ground in a park last night."

He turned to face away from her. The whole back was a sculpture of swollen muscle. "Yes, then please go ahead and wash me."

Rolling back the sleeves of her sweater, she squirted out a palmful of gel. Then she took the showerhead from its holder and ran the spray back and forth to his slender waist. Pausing to admire, she doused his proud buttocks as well.

Replacing the head, she spread the soap onto her hands and started to lather. Everything was velvety smooth as her palms glided in circular motions over his soft skin. This was far more delicious than ice cream. "Is that ok?" she asked, stifling a hiccup.

His voice was low. "It feels so good. Your hands are so soft."

Ogling his bottom, she tried to sound clinical. "Shall I wash all of the back of you?"

"Yes, please. You're the kindest host ever."

Running her hands along his shoulder blades, she collected foam and began covering his backside, massaging it along contours, admiring firmness. Breath becoming rapid, she found herself sliding her hand into the crack, reaching deep between his buttocks and soaping his asshole. There was a loud squidging of slippery skin as she rubbed her hand where even strong African sunshine couldn't reach.

"Is that ok? Not too much soap, I hope?"

He let out a slow sigh, almost whispering, "It's absolutely fine. You are just being...thorough."

"Well, I think I should be. Young men like you need to have clean bottoms, don't you?" The question was brazen, but naughty felt so nice.

"Yes, we do." He let out a soft moan as her fingertip massaged his tight rim.

"Good boy. You're all clean back here. I'll rinse you off." She aimed the jet and began washing away bubbles. Letting the water collect in her palm, she parted his smooth bottom cheeks and splashed between them. Five times. "Is the water warm enough? I forgot to ask. So rude of me, sorry."

"It's perfect. No need to apologize," he replied in a mellow, almost inaudible tone.

"Ok then, that's your back all done."

He turned; unable to meet her eyes. Coconut and pineapple fragrances were mixing with steam. His body was a toned block of gleaming wet muscle. Bashful hands covered his crotch, which he was pulling inwards, away from her. "I'm really so sorry. I feel very embarrassed. How rude of me." He was doubling over, but not in pain. Concealment was the aim of his awkward stance.

How lovely. This gorgeous man was aroused through no fault of his own, and yet he was being modest. "Oh, come on, what did I say before?"

"I have nothing to be ashamed of."

"Exactly. Now don't be silly. You can move your hands; it's fine."

All six feet of him straightened, moving his hands to his sides, and, as he did so, his enormous manhood was revealed in its erect glory. Loose hanging balls had reformed into a tight sack underneath the shaft, which twitched and pulsed with vitality. She judged it to be around 11 inches. About a foot of rock-hard male organ.

Panties now soaked; her heart was doing jumping jacks. Never mind the wine, she needed a brandy. With a deep inhale, she stepped forward, and, with her whole arm trembling, began fondling his bulbous scrotum.

"Don't be embarrassed. As you said, you're healthy…as a horse."

∞∞∞

Janice woke the next morning with a mouth screaming for saliva. Her tonsils felt like space hoppers. She must have been snoring like a chainsaw the whole night. She leaned over and slurped from a mug of water; her tongue welcomed the cool liquid as if it were a monsoon drenching the Sahara.

And bloody hell, her head. Was she wearing one of her woolly berets? Internally. This would be a lazy day, even by lockdown standards.

"Good morning," said a soft voice. Rolling over onto her side, she was met with Aaron's kind eyes. He was sat in bed wearing her black pyjama t-shirt with the duvet folded at his waist. Browsing through what looked like social media, he clicked his phone shut and said, "I hope you don't mind, but I took the wifi password from the back of your router."

"That's ok. What time is it?" she murmured.

He glanced at his phone. "Ten fifteen. How are you feeling?"

"Rough. But I seem to remember you persuading me not to have that final glass. Thank you."

"It's ok. I put it in the fridge for you. Can I get you some more water? And is there anything else you need? Please rest in bed and let me tend you."

"Some water would be great. Can you go to the fridge and bring the whole big bottle? And in that drawer over there I've got paracetamol. It's a blue packet. Can I have them please?" She lifted her head, turned the pillow, and lay her cheek on the cool cotton. A hint of peach fabric softener stroked her nostrils.

"Sure." Reaching over and pecking her forehead, he drew back the duvet and stood. She was thankful he had the pyjama trousers on too. Her hangover-addled brain didn't need visual reminders of what she'd done.

He put the painkillers on her bedside and walked to the door. As he opened it, she groaned, "And Aaron."

"Yes?"

"Pour that glass of wine down the sink."

Giving an empathetic look, he nodded before heading down the stairs.

Half a litre of water, two paracetamols, a banana, a vomit session, and extended snooze later, she was still feeling fragile, but at least the existential angst had faded. His caring nature had become clear. He'd knelt and rubbed her back while she projected semi-digested Thai curry mixed with sour red wine into the toilet bowl.

There was no doubt he had a good heart. If he'd been at least twenty years older and a proper boyfriend, the previous night's events would have been acceptable. As it stood, what had happened made her uneasy. Respectable women just didn't behave that way. Lockdown's pent-up frustration and loneliness had combined with far too much alcohol. She'd taken advantage of a young man who she was supposed to be offering a safe roof to. What had happened was a mistake and wouldn't be repeated.

She'd woken the second time to him stroking her head and gazing with his mocha browns. "Your blonde hair is very beautiful."

She took a glug from her water bottle. The thirst was mild now, but her throat still felt as if it had been assaulted with a cheese grater.

Taking away his hand, she said, "Aaron, I think we should talk about my behaviour last night."

He moved his body further down, turned on his side and rested head in hand. They were now lying face to face. "Sure, let's talk," he said with a bright-eyed smile.

"Well, I had far too much to drink, and, I need to say that I wouldn't normally do"—she paused— "those things with someone I've just met. Especially, not a boy of your age, because—"

"Why not?" he asked, with his forehead wrinkling.

"Because, for one thing, I'm not the kind of woman that goes to bed with strangers. I respect myself more than that." Adjusting the pillow under her arm and pulling the duvet higher, she realized this wasn't the best place to make such a statement.

His face was in a mild grimace, the beautiful eyes open wide. "But I respect you too. Very much. I don't understand?"

She rubbed his forearm. "I know you respect me, but...oh, never mind." As a 23-year-old boy, he wasn't going to understand. She'd press a different point. "Look, I'm old enough to be your mum, ok?"

"So?"

"So? So?"—flabbergasted, she hesitated— "So it means it's wrong, ok? I'm not a cradle snatcher, thank you very much."

He chuckled, "I'm not a child. You are not taking advantage of me. And what's a cradle?"

"It's a small bed for babies. You know the kind that go side to side?"

"Oh ok. Yes, I see. Well, I'm a grown man. My dick wouldn't even fit in a cradle."

She tutted, feigning annoyance, while having an internal giggle. "Don't be"—she struggled to find another word— "erm, cocky. Now, I'm happy for you to stay here until you can go back to Barbados, but I'd like us to be simply good friends, ok?"

He sighed, stroking her head again. She didn't stop him.

"Well, if that's what you want, I respect your decision. But can I just say one last thing? You're beautiful."

She scoffed, "Beautiful? I'm fat."

"You're a little chubby, that's all," he replied, rolling his eyes.

She shook her head in playful exasperation. Why did he have to be so bloody adorable? "Ok then, agreed? Friends?"

He smiled. "Friends."

"Ok, good."

"How are you feeling now?"

She let out a long exhalation. "My stomach's ok, but my head and throat are still not great. I have no energy."

"May I make you a sandwich? Soup? I will be sure to wash my hands for 20 seconds."

"You're so sweet. I think I should just drink water for now though and keep resting."

He pointed to the 32-inch TV on the wall. "How about we watch some movies and you can cuddle into me?"

"Cuddle?"

"You're sick, and I want to comfort you. Friends aren't allowed to comfort each other?"

"Well, they are, I suppose..."

"Then come here, please. You can choose all the movies." He opened his arms and gestured for her to lie with him.

She rolled over in the opposite direction. Then opened the top drawer of her bedside table, took out the TV remote control, and had another large gulp from her water bottle. "Ok, but I'm trusting you to be a gentleman," she said while turning on the TV and switching it to her favourite movie channel.

"Don't worry"—his eyes gestured south— "he's self-isolating today."

Unable to contain a smirk, she handed him the remote and eased herself into his embrace, sliding one arm across his waist and the other through the gap between his back and the two bulky pillows behind him. Wearing only panties and a thin vest, she overlapped her left leg across his and rubbed her bare sole against the bridge of his foot. It was smooth and warm. Well done, Janice, you've asserted your moral stance.

She couldn't deny it though. His strong arms made her feel so safe. As he flicked through the channels, with the jingle music of the movie channel humming in the background, he asked, "What kind of movie would you like to watch?"

"You choose. I think I'll sleep again anyway. Just don't turn the volume up."

Nestling into his manly chest, she continued to enjoy the smoothness of his feet.

Closing her eyes, she mumbled, "I'll do your laundry tomorrow, I promise."

Soft lips pressed against her forehead. "Thanks, dear. You're so kind." The lilt of his accent was soothing her headache.

"Frie—" She stopped herself. He was just being sweet, and this wasn't the most unpleasant way to recover from a drinking session.

As she snuggled into her human pillow, somewhere between consciousness and sleep, her mind drifted back to the previous night. She was still shocked at the debauchery. Her booze-soaked hormones had damp-dusted themselves off for an unexpected lockdown party. With all pretence at decency evaporated, she had indulged herself as Aaron stood soapy and erect in the tub.

∞∞∞

"Gosh, you've got big testicles, don't you?" she purred, kneading the fluffy skin of his sack between her thumb and fingers. Unlike her, it was the only part of his body which was wrinkly.

Head to the side, eyes half-closed, mouth agape, he was able to grunt a "Yeah."

"Do you like older women?"

"Yes, I like."

She took the showerhead, sprayed him across his front from head to toe, and said, "I think you're nice and clean now. I'm going to lead you into my bedroom by the penis. Is that a problem?"

"Your house. You do what you like."

"Good answer." She grasped his cock around the middle of the shaft with one hand and bid him to step out. Then she took a towel from the shelf and gave him a quick drying. That finished, her hand wrapped around his member again in a firm clasp as she led him across the hallway. Hot steam and brightness in the bathroom were replaced by cool air and dull yellow hue of dimmer lights set low.

Standing beside the bed, he asked, "Can I"—he motioned to her chest— "Can I see?"

Fuck it, belly damned. Pulling off her sweater, she was filled with delight to see his eyeballs bulge.

She ran fingertips over the front of her oversized beige bra. It had been more than a decade since she'd felt so sexy. "Do you want me to take this off?"

He swallowed hard, his breathing shallow as he nodded and said, "Yes, please. If you don't mind."

She rubbed soft beard and pinched his cheek. "You're a gentleman, aren't you?" She unclasped her bra and let it fall to the ground, stepping closer and putting her arms to her sides so he could have an unobstructed view.

His chest was rising and falling now; the cock swollen from blood flow. "Can I suck them?"

"Yes, suck."

He lifted her right breast—pausing to marvel at the size of it

—and placed his lips over the nipple and areola. She felt his whiskers tickle as he tried to fit in the whole thing. Greedy, gasping, his hands massaging, caressing, saliva bubbled and dripped as he slurped and licked. She held the spongy, soft curls of his crown, tilted his head to one side, and dipped her tongue into his ear, exploring the canal, sucking the lobe, biting around the shell.

She whispered, "Do you like sucking my breasts?"

Raising his head; lips and chin glistening, he replied, "I love it."

His breath was heavy as their tongues intertwined, their faces joined, feeding, jostling. "Do you want"—she kissed him hard on the lips— "to eat?"

"I will eat whatever my host puts in front of me."

Shaking, burning, shameless, she pulled down her jogging bottoms and knickers in one motion and kicked them into the corner. Lying on the bed and spreading her legs wide, she pointed her toes outwards and waited.

No prompting was needed. He gorged. Mouth dripping, head bobbing, the keenness of his youth proven as he probed; relentless, hungry, passionate. Tongue circled and flicked her clit as she squealed at delights from ravenous lips, slick with spit.

Grasping at his hair, eyes rolling to the ceiling, she contorted, writhed, her arms flailing, fingernails tearing at the duvet, clutching her own breasts, anything to help her as she spiralled out of her senses. She was ready. "Aaron, stop!"

"Are you ok?"

The reply was blunt: "Fuck me."

Wiping the drool, he kneeled on the bed, his penis so long he had to support it as he guided the tip towards her beckoning sex. But when he drew close, the penetration beginning, she placed a trembling palm on his six-pack and said, "No. I want doggy style."

He moved back to give her room. She turned onto knees, planted her face on the pillow and gave in to her femininity without reserve. "Grab my hips tightly. Slap my ass as hard as you like. Fuck me with that thing."

She let out a high-pitched gasp as his enormous cock slid in as far as her body could accept, stretching her limits, physical and mental. Biting on the soft cotton casing, Janice squealed as an iron grip held her hips, pumping, hammering, delving; challenging, the thrusts of his groin singing out loud slaps as it collided with her buttocks. Tears of ecstasy moistened the pillowcase. Knees shaking, heart racing, she reared her head and cummed, crying out, her essence releasing. And again. And again. And again.

She reached back and pushed his thigh away from her. She couldn't take any more. "Stop, sweety," she said, exhausted. Collapsing on her back, the bedcovers damp, her body filmed in perspiration, she invited him to cum all over her tits.

And he did. Hot jets of thick, gushing goo spurted across her upper body, overreaching onto her chin. One grazed her lips; she tasted salt and mineral stickiness. It was liquid life.

Puffing, spent, he lay beside her. "Was it nice?"

"It was amazing. Thank you. Thank you."

He cleaned the semen from her. They drank wine. Deep sleep followed.

∞∞∞

Aaron stayed for another week before he managed to arrange a replacement ticket. There was no more sex after that first night, but they continued to share a bed and friendship. He had a place in her heart, but conscience wouldn't allow her to repeat that first instance of soapy lust in lockdown, no matter how liberating it was. He'd made her realize she wasn't as old and fat as she thought, but she was still too mature to make a habit of cavorting with young boys. That just wasn't Janice.

They'd had glazed eyes when it came time to say farewell, but there was a consoling unspoken recognition of how special his stay had been. It was a one-time event, but that didn't reduce its profundity. The fond memories would fade, but never be forgotten.

Another week after Aaron left, the government announced an easing of restrictions. Kids went back to school, in half classes and shifts, to aid social distancing, and Janice returned with them. Her spa re-opened and with it the joy of plunging into a pool every evening. She was able to socialize again with her sisters, to neither of whom she mentioned about her Scouting for Couches guest from Barbados. They would not have approved.

Life was going to continue. Within the parameters of a new normal everyone talked about, but it would go on. That was the most important thing.

And it would do so with a new goal. She had decided to look for someone special to share her future with. Even if it took another ten years, Janice would be keeping an eye out, because the pandemic had taught that we never know what will happen.

That man, whoever he ended up being, wouldn't have the body of a demi-God, but he'd be there to give the affection missing in her life. She hoped their paths would cross soon.

Oil

~Canada, Present day~

Every sentence drawn out. One hundred words where one would suffice. Every fucking time.

"So, is that a yes or a no?" asked Evelyn with a long sigh. Her putty stress ball was taking a mashing. Squidgy pink material squeaked through her strong fingers, only to suck itself back for further squeezing when she reduced the pressure. She sometimes imagined it was a scrotum.

"Well, I would think yes. Most likely yes. I haven't been able to correlate all the data yet. Obviously, if you wanted to examine it and then decided the market was too uncertain, we would reconsider our approach. That would make it a no, of course," replied Nathaniel, her head of market research. Simpering weasel.

He was good at his job. Hence the reason he still had it. But she considered conciseness a virtue; in which he was lacking. Ditto with backbone. She hated these monthly one-to-one meetings with the department managers. Most of the information could be summarized in emails, but these guys—Nathaniel being one of the worst offenders—insisted on plodding through data in person. A sense of duty to the shareholders kept her in agreement. And from screaming.

Leaning into rich leather, she took in deep breaths. Her office was bigger than most apartments, with a panoramic view of the city, so why did she feel so fucking trapped? "It's Friday evening, Nathaniel. I'm tired. I'm sure you are too. And I'm sure you'll do a perfect job of correlating the data and making sensible recommendations from it. Can you please just send me a summary by email on Tuesday morning?"

"Well, I can send it to you before then if—"

"Tuesday morning is fine. Now if there's nothing else I'd like to try and enjoy the holiday weekend."

"I just wanted to ask ab—"

"Is it essential?"

"Well, I wouldn't say essential, perhaps. But we might—"

"That'll be all thank you. Have a nice weekend," she said, putting the putty toy into her desk drawer before swiping open her phone. Off he scurried. Evelyn wasn't a man-hater, but she despised ass kissers like him. A substantial proportion of the workforce seemed to be within that category. Evidence of the legacy left by the company's founder, her father. She was nowhere near as temperamental, which kept employee turnover—and blood pressure—far more stable than under her dad's reign.

Asserting authority was still important though, especially as a female CEO of African descent. But sometimes she wanted to receive a little more feistiness. The only guy employee she had an enjoyable rapport with was Samuel, the elderly security guard who manned the parking lot's boom gate booth. Well over 70 years old and frail, she should have had him replaced years ago—it wasn't like he was going to tackle any intruders—but he sassed like a grouchy grandfather and it made her chuckle.

She rotated her neck and stretched back and forth in a rowing motion. Too much sitting was murderous for muscles. It was unlikely, but she'd see if Karangasem—the most luxurious spa in the city—had any slots available. Being CEO of Baker Industries wasn't without its sacrifices, but it did mean she could afford to pamper herself whenever the chance came. At the end of her third consecutive 60-hour week in a month, a massage wasn't spoiling herself. It was medicinal.

"Good evening, Karangasem. Kirstin speaking, how can I help?"

"Hi there, Kirstin. This is Evelyn Baker. Do you have a therapist available for this evening?"

"Oh, hi Ms Baker. Nice to hear from you again. I'm fairly sure we're booked up tonight, I'm afraid. Let me double check. If you just give me one second"—elongated, hesitant syllables told Evelyn the booking diary was being scanned as they spoke— "hmm no...Oh, actually yes. We have a last-minute cancellation. Dakota has a slot available between 7pm and 9pm. Does that work for you?"

"Fantastic. Yes, it does."

"And what treatment are you looking for this evening?"

"Balinese massage. 2 hours."

"Ok, great. That's it booked then. See you at 7, Ms Baker."

∞∞∞

Evelyn parked her SUV within the white blankets of Karangasem's congested parking lot. Flakes were falling thick and fluffy; the breeze mild but still giving enough reason to tug her cashmere scarf tighter. Powdery snow collapsed in satisfying crunches under foot as she strode through fluttering haze. So pretty to look at, but her eyelashes were already being overwhelmed by delicate melting kisses. This type of weather was best enjoyed from indoors.

Stepping into the spa's welcoming serenity, she brushed off remnants of snowflake, cleaning her ankle boots with solid stamps. Chilly wind was replaced by warm caressing air as she removed the damp scarf. Soft panpipes and windchimes tootled and tinkled. The clean, fresh scent of peppermint was pervading. How nice to be away from that fucking office and all its toadies.

The reception and waiting area resembled a 5-star boutique hotel lobby. Fine leather, polished marble and well-watered plants. Ladies flicked through phones, magazines and treatment brochures, sipping on clay cups lifted from teak coasters.

"Ms Baker, so good to see you. Not the best night for driving, eh?"

"Hello, Kirstin. Yes, this weather constantly reminds me of why I have a 4x4."

Standing 5'11 without heels, she towered over the petite receptionist. Evelyn's busty, plump build contrasted with the slight frame of the pretty blonde girl. Full-figured but not obese, at 50 years old she was fitter than most women in their 20s. Decades of Taekwondo had been worth the investment.

"It was a smart choice, but then if anybody knows cars…"

"Fair point," she replied with a modest nod.

"So, Dakota will be with you in just a minute. He's quite new here, but I think you'll find he's a fantastic therapist."

"He?"

Kirstin looked awkward. "Yes…didn't I mention? He's our new male therapist"—she cleared her throat— "he's very good though. Has great feedback."

"I just assumed Dakota was a female."

"I'm so sorry. We've been busy all day and I've been run ragged. I should have checked with you. Is it a problem?"

"Well, I supp—"

"Hey," said a voice to her side. She turned to find herself looking at a man of extraordinary good looks. Pecs and biceps bulging under a white spa uniform polo; his tanned, square chin was peppered in jet black stubble. At around 6'2, the hazel eyes, dimples and suave spiked hair—black with crimson highlights—had her saying, "Dakota? I'm Evelyn. Nice to meet you. So, lead on."

∞∞∞

Nude except for a soft cotton towel draped across her behind, she was having tension expelled from her system at a rapid rate. Dakota was making a wonderful first impression. Respectful but not subservient, he was soothing skin in smooth sweeps and kneading muscle with gentle but firm presses. His hands were robust and manly, but the palms soft and caring. The oil being rubbed on her body was luxuriant in its rich radiance of—what smelled like —blended lavender, lemongrass and ylang ylang.

In blissful trance, she was slumbering, her whole body heavy and glowing. She was wet too. Not dripping, but moist. Promising herself to find more time for regular treatments, she bathed in the pleasure brought by masculine touch from head to toe.

"How are you feeling? Everything ok?" His low whispering sent delightful tingles throughout her body.

"More than ok. Perfect." Her eyes were closed; the words oozed out.

"So glad to hear that."

"Sorry I didn't put on the paper panties. They were a little too small. You know, I'm not exactly a skinny woman."

"Are you fishing for compliments, madam?" His tone and delivery were the perfect balance of familiarity and professionalism.

She gave a sleepy snort. "You're used to female clients then."

"Yep. And it's spa policy not to comment on clients' bodies"—she heard a gurgling squirt of oil before his splendid hands returned— "but no you're not skinny. Definitely not fat though. You have a wonderful figure, actually."

She hadn't had a welcome compliment from an attractive man in…She couldn't even remember when. Her ex-husband—divorced for 3 years now—wasn't much for affectionate words. And all she got at work was disingenuous flattery.

"Really?" She wanted all kinds of pampering.

"Yes, you do. Very feminine and healthy. Do you want me to work on your glutes?"

"Yes, please." She was feeling like that putty ball. Soft and not capable of resistance.

The towel drawn to the middle of her buttocks; silky hands slid across the sides of her bottom in tender glides. Yum. She could feel air against her vagina and hoped he was able to get a peek.

"How old are you?"

"I just turned 32 last week."

Noting his politeness in not returning the question, she murmured, "I feel so old compared to you."

"More fishing?" They laughed.

Knowing she had a rare long weekend ahead, a thought occurred. "Do you feel my muscles are quite knotted?"

"I'd say so, to be honest. A lot of stress at work?"

"Yes, and too much sitting. Would you recommend a course of treatments?"

"I'm a broke massage therapist, I always recommend treatment."

She smiled. "Tell me more about yourself."

∞∞∞

After roundabout questions which had confirmed he was neither married nor gay, Evelyn had persuaded Dakota to come to her home for an outcall massage session the next day. He'd been unsure about breaking Karangasem's rules—which forbade their clients becoming private ones—but adding to the pot for his master's degree in physiotherapy had swung it. He'd agreed, but upon her promise not to mention it to anyone.

He needn't have worried. She had her own prerogative about discretion. A document lay on the coffee table in her cavernous living room, weighted against the glass surface by a chic designer pen. Nothing would happen without him signing.

Her phone rang. It was gate security. "Hello? Yes, it's ok, he's my therapist. Let him through. Yes, thank you."

Sandra, her live-in home manager, was abroad, enjoying a luxury ski chalet in the Rockies—courtesy of Evelyn—so it was herself who padded across gleaming white marble to answer the doorbell when it rang. Were the scarlet silk pyjamas too direct? She hoped so.

"Hi Dakota, I hope you didn't have any trouble finding the house." He stood on the top doorstep with his folding massage table and backpack. Puffy duck-down jacket shielding him from the elements; lazy snowfall was making occasional deposits on his crimson-streaked shock. The stubble was still there, coated around a cheeky smile. Fucking stud.

"This place is really something," he said, putting down his gear and taking in the lofty ceilings and decadent Feng shui. "I mean, I was expecting luxury but"—he let out a weak whistle—"this is something else. No wonder though, considering."

"Thanks. Let me take your jacket. Come, sit down. I'd like to discuss something with you," she said, gesturing to the central suite area.

As he sat, she reached over the living room bar and grabbed a swollen manila envelope. "Take it."

He did. "And...what's this?"

"5,000 dollars. Cash."

"I see"—he leaned across leather with a hint of cockiness—"You do realise my fee for massage is only 50 an hour, right?"

She smiled, walking behind the bar. Rows of premium and rare liquor bottles lined the shiny glass shelves; the booze crammed together in a variety rivalling most pubs or nightclubs. There were even three kinds of draft beer on tap. And she hardly drank; it was there for decoration and vanity more than anything else. "Want a drink?"

"Do you insist?"

"I'd like you to relax, although I don't like to insist with...friends."

"Friends? Yes, I suppose we are friends. I'll take a beer then, thanks. Give me a large"—his finger teetered between Evelyn and the badged brass tap beside her— "glass of that thick creamy black one. Thanks a lot."

Pouring, she pointed to the coffee table. "Check that paper. Tell me what you think."

"Non-disclosure. It says I can't tell anyone what happens in our therapy sessions. Do you really like to keep your massages that secret?" She handed him the stout and he sipped, taking in the opulence of exquisite furnishings and art.

"I think you understand the situation. Although not entirely."

"Well, you're not the first woman from the spa who's asked for...private therapy, although you are by far the richest and"— he took a glug of the beer— "that's tasty. There's just something about the black stuff, isn't there?"

"I like to speak directly. I'd like the same in return, please. Let's lose the innuendo."

"Ok, so...what exactly do you want?"

"I want to be put in my place."

He put his drink on the tabletop with a gentle clink and leaned forward, resting elbows on knees. Biceps swelled under tanned skin as he did so. Plain red cotton was drawn tight against sinew. "Put in your place? Can you be more specific...?"

"Bossed around, told to obey, used sexually..."

His cheeks moulded into dimples; the lips parting to reveal pearls in perfect alignment. "You want me to use you, sexually?"

"Yes. But boss me about too."

"Is this what you normally ask your therapists to do?"

"All I need to hear is yes or no from you. Long answers irritate me. So, yes or no?"

He opened the envelope and rasped his thumb down the crisp bills as if they were cards about to be dealt. "Yes. If this is for one session"—he leaned back and gestured around the room with his eyes— "as something tells me I need the money more than you do."

"Fine. If you do a satisfactory job today, I might make it a regular thing. You'll be able to pay for a PhD on top of your master's. Sign, please."

After storing the NDA in a secure filing cabinet, she returned to find him looking out of the living room's floor-to-ceiling windows; his broad back tapering to a V-shape as he stood with hands on hips. Feathery snow was now cascading in flurries over the landscaped gardens. They'd been transformed into an enormous carpet of lumpy cotton wool. Without turning, he said, "Beautiful, isn't it? Your garden is as big as my whole neighbourhood. Nice high walls you've got too. It must be great, to be able to shut out the world and all its problems."

"I bring them home just like anyone else. But I'd like you to give me a break from them."

He turned. "So, what are the rules?"

"The safe word is 'unicorn'."

"Ok, anything else."

"What's the safe word? Say it three times."

"Unicorn"—he took a step closer— "unicorn"—closer still — "unicorn." Their noses were now a few inches apart. Cheap supermarket deodorant was wafting from his armpits. Mixed with rugged muskiness, it rivalled any niche designer fragrance.

"If I say the safe word, you stop immediately."

Brushing dangling blades of long black fringe from her forehead, he replied, "Ok. Any other rules?"

"No violence at all. Not even a slap. That clear?"

He nodded. "Fine. Is that it?"

"Yes"—she squeezed his solid bicep— "put me in my place. Begin."

Sitting down again, he stroked his stubbly chin in thought and sipped the beer. He told her to sit. "So, the non-disclosure. It cuts both ways, right?"

"Yes, it does."

"That's yes, sir."

Adrenaline slapped her stomach. "Yes, sir."

"Good. Call me sir every time, ok?"

"Yes, sir." Those words had become almost foreign language, spoken in that context. It was exhilarating to hear them revived, firing from her lips. Like linguistic slumming.

"Good girl. Move back a little. We need room. So, as you know, I massage women. Almost all my clients are women. Different shapes, heights, colours and scents. But one thing wealthy ladies seem to have in common is their pretty, painted feet. Take off your socks."

No arguments, no questions, just obedience. Feeling a wonderful sense of freedom, she slipped off her thin black socks to reveal glossy, pampered toes. The result of regular—and expensive—pedicures.

He clicked his fingers, pointed to her feet and beckoned. "Give."

His palm was still smooth but the grip tighter than it had been in Karangasem. Cupping her sole, he sat forward and began licking the bridge with a wide tongue. The wet flesh sliding in repeated laps across her skin was warm and invigorating, sending ripples of shivering delight along her legs and beyond.

He took his time. Stubble scratched like sandpaper as he slurped, kissed and sucked. Her feet became shiny with saliva. And they weren't the only part feeling sticky.

"Come closer"—he began unbuttoning the jacket of her pyjamas— "you've obviously got big tits, but I want to see exactly how big."

So rude. Devilish. She was being further unburdened. Not just of clothing, but the constant weights of authority and responsibility. All she had to do was obey.

Sliding the silk top from her shoulders, he folded and tossed it on the coffee table. Her E cup breasts were hanging bare. She'd been told not to cover. The air was lukewarm against her skin as he inspected them, smiling.

He was blunt in his words. "You've got very big tits, don't you?"

"Yes, sir." Even the effort of answering was minimal. Heaven.

Taking them in his hands, he groped, squeezing her nipples and areola between index fingers and thumbs, pinching them. She let out gasps; the sensations blurring between soft pain and strong pleasure.

With a palm placed under her left breast, he pressed up and down in a weighing action. "Heavy. Do you think there's milk in there?"

"No, sir."

He licked his index finger and smirked. "Let's double check, shall we?" His fingertip teased in delicious tickling circles around her nipples, which rose bigger and harder until both stood proud like pencil erasers. Squeezing so the tops were peaked, he said, "I doubt I'll get a whole tit in my mouth, but I'll try."

Insatiable sucking and nibbling had Evelyn struggling. Arms behind her back—as she'd been ordered—he gorged in groans, grunts and moans; she was grimacing, panting, desperate to dig her nails into scalp, to chew on ear lobe. But she wasn't allowed. It was beautiful torture.

The feast continued. Her panties were starting to soak.

"I was hoping to tease some milk out of you. Never mind." Standing, he unzipped his jeans and pulled them to the bottom of his groin. Then his white boxer briefs. His flaccid cock hung huge, thick; the crotch a couple of shades lighter than his dark caramel thigh tops. "Go down on your knees. Suck my cock."

She hadn't done that for years. And she had to be really into a guy to do it. Dakota was a fox. Not a problem.

She was on her knees, topless in 1500-dollar pyjamas. "Of course, sir"—she stroked the black hair of his ball sack— "may I suck your balls too, please?"

He petted her head, running his fingers over her silky crown. "Yes, you may. But only because you asked politely."

"I am—"

"Shhh"—he placed a finger across his lips— "suck."

Gobbling his large testicles one at a time, she rolled them, massaging with lips and tongue; the pulls on his sack ending with energetic pops. Gourmet salt from soft hair and crinkled skin graced her tastebuds. Tender time was spent indulging in the pleasure of a real man's balls.

Cock was next to be devoured. Fully inflated, the shaft was straight with a swollen head of maroon. Must have been 8 or 9 inches. She ran her tongue around the helmet, savouring its smooth texture and drawing satisfaction from his moans. The thing was too long to swallow whole, but she did her best to suckle his prick with generous dribble and spit.

"Very nice. You're a sweet little cocksucker, aren't you?" he asked, running his fingers through her fringe. It was an outrageous question. But—considering the circumstances—a valid observation.

"Yes, sir."

"Say it then."

"I'm a sweet little cocksucker," she squeaked. Degrading. Delicious.

After extended time giving her best blowjob, he said through gritted teeth, "Good girl. I think I'm ready for something more."

She was told to stand and go to the window. "Face outside. Don't look at me. And if you want to talk, put your hand up to ask permission." The enormous Persian rug was soft on soles as she walked across it in compliance. Snow was still tumbling, swirling in brilliant haze. Goosepimples were prickling her skin, but not from cold.

"Take off those pyjama trousers. Now."

Off they came. It was so simple. He said and she did. Hands came from behind and yanked her French cut designer panties to her ankles. She was standing stark naked.

"So, how do you like to be fucked?" Breath from his whisper warmed her earlobe. Words slithered; eardrum quivered.

"Doggy, sir."

He scoffed, rubbing her buttocks in circular motions, clasping the flesh, patting and tapping. "I might have known. What is it about women and doggy? Fine then."

Only allowed to look straight ahead, she heard the plastic hiss of a bag zip, then rustle and clink of clothing. He was naked too.

"May I see you please, sir?"

"Beg."

"Please, sir."

"Beg louder."

"Please, sir!"

He laughed. "Fine. Turn and face me then. I won't deny you the pleasure of looking."

Oh my God. She was met with Adonis, reborn. Abdominals, pectorals, biceps, triceps; every sculpted section was defined in protruding blocks, natural plate armour pushing from underneath tanned skin. His Herculean chest was smooth, flawless, the shoulders bumpy with muscle, flickering, flexing. Thighs and calves of a Spartan were twined with sinew and wrapped in raven hair. His latex-sheathed cock was pointing straight, pulsing, twitching. Hungry and ready to feed.

And she was the meal. "Fuck me please, sir."

Placing a hand on her shoulder, he marched her through to the dining area and its table. One swipe sent a flower-filled crystal vase tumbling onto varnished oak floor in sharp, chiming shatters. The tablecloth was pulled and thrown to one side as he bent her over the edge. "Stick your ass up. Further. We're going to fuck, you know!"

His diamond-hard length nestled between her lips. Pushing them apart, it began to slide deep. She let out a yelp and slammed the table's surface with the heel of her hand; it was almost too much cock to cope with. Fully stretched, she squealed as he pumped with palms fastened tightly on her hips, hammering, belting; her pussy dripping, melting, fizzing from his manhood continually ramming and retreating, prodding and probing. She rubbed her clit in determined rhythm, moving the fingers fast; focused on glorious release.

Knees trembling, her gasps became groans. Strong pulses of pleasure translated to loud shouts, cries, as the table rattled and creaked with every thrust of his enormous cock into her wet and welcoming crotch. Their skin slapping, one hand clamped on her tit, squeezing, kneading; her nerves were alight, bleeding. She couldn't hold on. Multiple screams blended into one, broken by desperate gasps for air as she unleashed a series of riotous orgasms which echoed throughout the mansion's decadent halls.

Gasping, she tapped his thigh. "Enough, honey. I can't cum

more."

He eased out. Evelyn turned to see the condom's tip was bloated and sagging from all the semen encased within. His balls had an impressive reservoir.

She steadied herself on his broad chest, exhausted. Panting, he asked with a smile, "Was it nice? Did you like it?"

"Like it? I"—she took several deep breaths— "loved it! You really put me in my place." They laughed.

"So, what should I do now? You want me to go? Or…?"

Squinting, she replied, "Go? Are you crazy? You brought a bunch of massage stuff, didn't you? Let's have lunch then"—she planted a loud slap on the firm flesh of his peachy ass— "you're breaking out that oil, boy."

∞∞∞

The following Tuesday, Evelyn was reclining in her office chair with a smile. She'd had the most amazing holiday. Not from boarding the private jet to visit beaches in Hawaii or go skiing in Colorado, but by taking a break from herself.

Head clear and muscles soothed, she opened her laptop to find Nathaniel's inevitable email. It had been sent first thing. She scanned its verbose message, picking out the essentials. His conclusion was astute, so she typed a quick reply telling him so and that she agreed. Simple.

She looked in the desk drawer at her stress ball. It was going to be getting less use from now on. Regular therapy sessions had already been arranged.

Flash Fiction Erotica: Milk

~France, Present day~

"I'll leave him in your capable hands, nurse."

"Thank you, doctor."

Dr Augustin's message was clinical. At least, the one leaving her lips was. The eyes smirked a different story from behind polished spectacle lenses as she stepped out of the room. Nurse Alice Claude was now in charge of the young gentleman laid on the bed under bright lights.

The doctor's examination had been brief. Stretching the patient's underwear elastic out to look inside, she'd needed less than a minute of inspection before deciding on the correct treatment. The words given as she exited had confirmed the necessary remedy.

"So, Raphael, before we get started, I'll just do a quick check of your blood pressure," said Alice with a kindly smile as brown hands wound black sleeve around white bicep. Fixing the bristled material in place, she grasped and squeezed the rubber ball pump. Fresh, natural; he smelled of cut grass, flecks of which were spattered on the outsoles of his expensive white sneakers.

"And that's fine. Slightly low, but it's ok. It's certainly not an issue for the next procedure."

Raphael, who had arrived in rigid distress, was captain of the university soccer team. Toned muscles slender, blonde hairstyle sharp and blue eyes tender; he was an adorable man of 21 years old. But his teammates were not as sweet, it seemed. He'd been pranked with erectile dysfunction medication in his sports drink. Resulting in the condition before her now. With his jeans unbuttoned and the fly spread wide, his green boxer briefs were struggling to contain the situation.

"And what's that, nurse?" His tone had calmed since his arrival—after Dr Augustin gave assurance his penis wouldn't explode—but Raphael still spoke with obvious discomfort. And no wonder. She'd help him though.

The velcro sleeve rasped as she unwound and removed it. "Penile manipulation."

"Penile—"

"I have to milk you, sweety."

"Milk?" Pale cheeks changed to pink.

She gave his forearm a delicate rub in reassurance. "Don't worry. It's a slightly uncommon procedure, but it's not painful. Quite the opposite, in fact. We need to empty these"—she laid two gentle fingers on his cotton-covered ball sack— "and the erection should subside soon after ejaculation. You're going to feel immense relief, I promise. It must have been a very low dose you got anyway. Believe me, it's not the emergency it seems. A good milking and you'll be fine."

"Well in that case...I mean, I'm not a child, nurse. Maybe I should do it myself?" Light blush in his face had strengthened to scarlet.

She pursed her lips, mulling. "Yes, you could. Although I've found on the other occasions this type of problem has"—she looked at the gigantic hard-on straining in its pouch— "sprung up, that relief is achieved far faster and more effectively with professional assistance. What do you think?"

"Well, if it gets this thing down quicker then maybe—"

"I think it's just better I milk you myself, so it's done properly, ok?"

Sucking in a deep breath, he said, "Ok, just please get rid of this pressure. It feels like stone and its aching really strongly."

"Don't worry, it'll be gone before you know it. Now, let's get you ready, shall we?" The rail gave a metallic buzz as she whisked the light green curtain, cloaking the bed and its immediate area. Taking hold of the open flaps of his jean flies, she tugged. "Ok, lift your butt, please. I'll just take them off so they're out of the way."

She removed his sneakers and socks and placed them underneath the bedside chair, on top of which she put his folded jeans and t-shirt. "Is it really necessary for me to be naked, nurse?"

"There's going to be liquid squirting, so yes, I think it's best if you're nude"—she patted the firm muscles of his thigh— "You don't want to go back outside in sticky clothes, do you?"

Instead of answering, he looked in agitation at his one remaining piece of clothing. The green material was stretched; a bulging ridge of masculine organ was desperate to escape its confines. "I feel so embarrassed."

Hooking her fingernails under the elastic band at the top, she said, "There's nothing to be embarrassed about. We see it all, believe me. Now can you move your bum while I take these off?"

She had to pull the front wide out so it could be manoeuvred over his swollen cock. As soon as the restraint of tight cotton was removed, it stuck straight in the air. A head of dark ruby sat atop its meaty white shaft, at the bottom of which were balls covered in straw-coloured blonde hair. Everything was huge. There was going to be mess.

After taking a discreet glance at his impressive physique, she plucked rubber gloves from a large box and drew both on with sharp snaps, interlocking her fingers to mould them tight. Lubricant gurgled from its tube as she squeezed a generous dollop into her palm. She rubbed her hands together, enjoying the lube's slimy texture. "I'll just make them warm for you"—she cupped, exhaled and rubbed again— "as I think that'll help things along quicker."

She sat next to him and took his dick in a gentle grasp. Greasy latex glistened in the light as she ensured the whole member was covered in goo. Speaking in a soft, melodious tone, her tongue slid over syllables as she commentated. "So, we'll just make sure the hat's fully covered"—she ran a fingertip in circular motions around his bulbous cock head— "and there, that's looking nice and shiny isn't it?" She noted the contrast between his forearm and hers: freckled porcelain beside flawless hickory.

"Are you ok so far?"

Raphael's eyes were closed. He nodded and let out a slow breath. "Yes, fine. Please continue, nurse."

"So"—her gloved grip glided the full length of his cock twice— "there we go. Think the shaft is suitably lubricated. There's no chafing, is there?"

"No, it's fine thanks." The volume of his voice had dropped further. She could see his ball sack had tightened against the base of his prick.

"Good. See? And you were nervous too. Nothing to be nervous about. We'll soon have you feeling better, won't we?"

"Yes."

"All we need now is a little elbow grease." She began slick slides up and down his dick, increasing the speed as he clasped the mattress and gritted his teeth. He was right. It was hard as stone. Poor gentleman. Relief was on its way though.

As latex squeaked and lube squidged, his eyes were averting as he started to make restrained gasps. She could sense him flitting between feelings of ecstasy and awkwardness. "Raphael, dear?"

"Yea?" His voice was murmured, trance-like.

"You're a man. It's ok to like this, ok? Just relax and enjoy. You'll get relief quicker if you do."

"Thank you." He reached out and began massaging her upper arm through crisp creases of pressed navy uniform, causing her ID badge to swing in gentle knocks as she worked his massive cock. "Is it ok?"

"Yea, its ok. You just tell me when you start getting the urge to release."

Breath accelerating, he opened his eyes and said, "Maybe…"

"Maybe what?"

"Maybe you could, you know"—he tapped his lips— "put my…if you wanted to, of course."

"Give you a?"—she tutted and gave his thigh a light slap— "I certainly cannot, young man. This isn't a date, you know."

They smiled. His given through pulses of pleasure, hers alongside understanding eyes.

Her hand began pumping fast. Faster still. His hold hardened around her arm as he gave out groans of increasing volume; the handsome face masked in torturous pressure. With her wrist going at full rate, it wouldn't be long. His balls had all but disappeared, retreated, ready to unload; Alice was curious to see how far their juices would jet.

"I think I'm gonna cum soon."

"Just let it all out, ok? Release it. Don't hold back. Do you want me to stop once you start cumming? Or go slow? Fast?"

"Slow, please. I'm gonna cum"—he tensed, his grip on her strengthening to iron— "I'm gonna cum!"

Pearly liquid frothed from his tip. Bubbling at first, then unleashing with a spurt that striped across rippling abdomen and twitching pectorals. And again. His balls began unleashing a torrent. Squirts loosed in sloppy succession, fresh, pent-up; he shouted out loud as his load landed in thick, sticky strings across the length of his upper body until they ended with an enormous sigh of relief. He lay back, exhausted, plastered in his own fluids.

Alice's gloved hand was coated, gleaming with lube and globules of warm cum. "There we go, all done. Fully milked and"—she gave the shaft a gentle tap— "see? It's going down already. How do you feel? You ok?"

"So good. Thank you so much. You're an amazing nurse."

"It was a pleasure." Although I'm more of a milkmaid today, she thought.

Teeth

~Colonial East Africa, 19th Century~

Booker opened the door to be met with nipples. At 6'3 he was eye level with them. That wasn't normal.

But then, neither was the size of the man they belonged to. A sycamore stood in the hallway. Fur loin cloths, jagged claw necklaces and machetes sheathed in leather told him the giant and his companion were tribal warriors. The question was why they were standing in front of his room.

Yawning—having woken a minute before—he rubbed his face in hopes of unsticking puckered eyelids.

"Mr Shaw? Are you Mr Booker Shaw, the hunter?" asked the much smaller guy with a clarity of English that took him by surprise.

The previous night at O' Malley's was still returning to him as his brain shooed cobwebs of hungover confusion from its casing, but he was sure there hadn't been any tribesmen at the poker table or even in the saloon. He couldn't owe them money or— even worse—a debt of honour, could he?

Keeping the rickety wooden door open a crack, he peered down, then craned his neck. What an odd-looking pair. The men, not the nipples.

"Depends. What do you want?" His mouth was like sandpaper. Damn, was he pining for a cold beer.

"Well we came to offer a proposal and"—he bent and stood presenting a clinking box— "we brought you these as a gift."

A half dozen pint bottles of British ale packed in loose ice. Crying with condensation. Thank you, God.

He slid the 45-calibre revolver in his left hand back into its holster on the desk. "Booker Shaw, at your service. Come on in. Mind your head, big fella."

He pulled on an undershirt and fastened his leather suspenders over it, before using the metal bed frame to pop the top from a beer. Sending the cap across creaky floorboards with a metallic tinkle, he caught the gushing froth and glugged, giving a thumbs up. The frosty bite of hop-filled fizz was a rejuvenation for his tongue and throat. He took the bottle from his lips with a gasp of satisfaction, saying, "I don't know why you fellas are here, but you are most"—he nodded at the now half-empty beer in his hand— "and I mean most, welcome. You want one?"

The small tribesman—who was in fact average size but looked smaller in relation to his company—replied with a smile, "You are so kind, Mr Shaw. We do not partake, thank you."

"That's a pity. Still, more for me. Why don't you fellas take a seat?" He motioned to two chairs beside the damp-riddled wall. Then he eased onto the window seat's grubby cushion and flipped the flimsy lock in search of less stale air. A breeze began to whisk in; warm but with enough force to aid in his revival. He continued to guzzle. Suds were supplying a cool internal massage. The sweat on his forehead no longer fierce; this day was turning out better than he'd expected.

The two men remained standing. Gesturing upwards with his hands, the man of lesser stature said, "Mr Shaw, my name is Obasi. May I introduce to you Prince Jaheem, son of Zuberi the king of the great nation of Yakanaka."

Unsure how to react, he tapped the bottle to his head as a salute. "Welcome, prince. I wasn't expecting royalty today. Does he speak English?"

The prince—whose head was brushing the ceiling of Booker's modest hotel room—sat on the unvarnished wooden chair nearest to him and nodded with a serious expression, before saying with a chuckle, "And extremely poor French."

He was relieved to hear good-natured laughter from the enormous man with the massive knife. The guy called Obasi chimed in with accompanying titter. Booker added his own guffaws. And they had a moment. He was already warming to them.

"So, to what do I owe this honour, your erm—"

"Please, just Jaheem. And it is I who have the honour of speaking to the legendary hunter, Booker Shaw from Ken-tu-kee."

Perching on a chair, Obasi said, "And my prince is also a great hunter. As am I."

"Great hunter? You?"—the huge man reared his head back and roared in laughter— "I wouldn't trust you to kill a chicken that was already dead." His banana-sized fingers spread over Obasi's bald head, giving it an affectionate rub. "You're a lucky mascot though. May the Sun continue to protect you."

With the first formalities dispensed, the prince and servant were teasing each other, bickering over muddled details of past animal encounters. This was fun. He swigged his free beer, enjoying the banter and billow of wind.

The street below was in peak traffic. Its moist ground muddy from sustained trudge; the sides were lined with sun-bleached wooden buildings and shacks of chaotic height and quality. Trappers guided mules laden with furs, soldiers swaggered; their red tunics buttoned in brass, traders clicked and flapped reins to steer their laden carts through the crowds while sweet, starchy whiffs of boiling rice and corn mingled with the salty smoke of barbecue; the meats best to remain anonymous if full satisfaction was sought.

He lifted another bottle from the box, shaking off excess drip before positioning the cap's crimped edge to open from a well-placed thump. The foam filled his mouth as he sucked it down. Most welcome, indeed. The two benevolent gentlemen had finished their playful argument and re-focused on him. Seemed like they were about to make their proposal. Problem was, he wanted to drink and chit chat, not talk about killing. At least, not yet.

"So, where did you gents learn English so well? You"—he pointed to Obasi— "speak better than half the folks in Kentucky.

And you"—he softened his tone, giving a polite nod and smile to the prince— "you're not bad either. Not bad at all."

Prince Jaheem turned to Obasi and said in light scorn, "Yes you're a language man, but enough clucking from you for now. You're like a wife, but without the fun. Let the big boys speak, ok?"

"Yes, my prince. And who is bigger than you?" Obasi gave a shrug and eye roll.

After raising eyebrows at his—supposed—obedient subject, he answered Booker. "Missionaries. My father in his wisdom allowed them to stay in our village with us. They taught us many things. Like to speak English. And I thank the Sun. I was never very capable, but because of my learning, I am at least able to talk with the great Booker Shaw."

"Your father does indeed sound wise," he replied, aware that despite being a so-called great hunter he was in the second cheapest hotel in Port Moranko. The least expensive had no vacancies. "So, you fellas are Christian then?"

The prince shook his head. "The rules didn't prove so popular. Especially with me. I had to choose between salvation and a harem of beautiful wives."

Booker tipped another bubbling mouthful. "You decided to go to hell happy."

"Exactly." Their laughter was joined by Obasi's.

"Hmm Yakanaka. Your people live on an island up north, right? In one of the great lakes? Or am I getting confused?"

"No. No confusion. We do indeed. The biggest island. Yakanaka Island in Lake Zvakawanda. Approximately 9,000 people live in our kingdom."

"Although the number is falling," muttered Obasi. There was no rebuttal from Prince Jaheem. He nodded confirmation. Humour had fizzled.

Booker leaned into the window seat and stretched his feet —clad in worn cream cotton—on the bed. Rusty springs squeaked under the weight of his thickly muscled legs. Wafts of corn were starting to tickle his belly. No point in checking his wallet. He wished he were better at poker. Or any damn card game.

"So, what exactly is the situation in your country, gentlemen?" he asked before swilling another fizzy gulp.

Jaheem leaned back, the chair—which his colossal legs made look like children's furniture—straining. With a tree branch arm, he motioned to scholarly Obasi.

"Not good, Mr Shaw," replied Obasi, sitting forward. Sullen, he spoke quickly. "Great tragedies have occurred. Many loved ones taken from us"—he grimaced, shaking his head in brief contemplation— "and as if this were not terrible enough, as an island nation we rely on fishing. Not only for food for our own people, but we also trade with the other tribes and sell to the British. Our land has rich soil and can grow many crops; we keep large numbers of cows, sheep and goats, but the lake is vital to our economy. The west side of Yakanaka is famed for its large fish and we catch many in our nets. They fetch an exceptionally fine price at market. But the fishing there has stopped."

He listened while caressing stubble on his chin and cheeks, feeling its prickly abrasion. "Problem's on the land? Or in the water?"

"Both."

"Crocodile or hippo?"

"Crocodile, but not like we've seen before."

"How so?"

"All accounts say it is at least two—perhaps three—times the size of a normal beast. Striking frequently, not only in the lake but also within the coastal fields. People have become afraid even to tend the crops in that area."

"How many has it taken?"

"In the four months since the attacks started, the monster has killed 48 of our people. Including"—he hesitated, looking at the prince— "including—"

"It killed my mother," said the prince. "She was bathing in the lake with her handmaidens and it dragged her down."

"I'm very sorry for your loss, Jaheem."

"Thank you, Mr Shaw. Yakanaka must be rid of this devil.

We need your help to kill it. That is our proposal."

Booker sighed, running his finger along the bottle's smooth rim. "I don't want to come across as insensitive, fellas, but it sounds mighty risky. And with risk I expect reward. What kind of payment can you offer?"

"500 silver Britannias," replied Jaheem. "Paid when the beast lies dead in front of me."

Concealing shock, he nodded and pursed his lips. "Sounds fair." The last job had paid 120, for a leopard which had almost clawed his nuts off. He could bait the croc in the right spot then blow its brains out from afar. If he kept time near the water's edge to a minimum and hunted in daylight, this would be easy money. Unlike leopards, crocodiles couldn't climb trees.

"Gentlemen, I accept your proposal."

Smiles broke from the two warriors. Their reaction was the same: "Thank the Sun."

"But may I ask—I mean I assume your warriors have tried—has there been any interaction with the croc from your own hunting attempts?"

Jaheem answered. "The Yakanaka are skilled with spear, arrow and knife, and most braves have claimed a lion or leopard"—he tapped at his claw necklace— "but this demon eludes our hunts. And we don't know if our spears and arrows would be sufficient. The few who have caught a glimpse of it say the size is terrifying, but that it also darts under the cover of water with great speed. That is why my father decided to seek you out."

"Seek me out, but not the colonel of the garrison outside town? He commands a thousand rifles." They seemed set on him doing the job, so he felt safe enquiring why they hadn't gone for other options.

The answer from Jaheem was blunt: "We do not want British soldiers on our land."

"All they know is plunder. We prefer our relationship with them not extend beyond trade in this city's markets. Our king does not want them roaming in our country. If you get into bed with the Devil, Mr Shaw, you will eventually find yourself shivering with no sheets," said Obasi.

"Hmm. I like that. Will need to remember that one. And I can assure you, gentlemen, that I have always believed in sharing the sheets."

"Your reputation as a man of honour and skill is unquestionable. That is why my father will be pleased to see you."

"And I him. Now, I don't suppose you fellas could advance me a couple of pennies, could you? My belly is crying out for some corn."

∞∞∞

Booker was used to being the biggest man in any given vicinity. Not so on Yakanaka Island. He was feeling average.

In terms of size. Popularity was a different matter. Smiles, whoops and buzz of excitement had met them as they'd crossed a sturdy timber bridge into the villages and hamlets of Yakanaka. Seemed like they hadn't seen a tall, handsome white man before. Had him blushing. Well, almost.

Feeling dandy with his khaki hunting outfit pressed and knee-high military boots polished; black steel revolvers were strapped on either side of his chest with the two holsters positioned horizontally for fast draw. They rarely saw action in a hunt for big game—45 not being a calibre suited to fast disposal of large animals—but their gleaming ivory and chrome handles looked mighty impressive.

All the guns and ammunition he'd actually use were stored in his new lodgings. And a fine tent it was too. In the posh part of town, as Obasi had put it. Large, in fact more so than the hotel room he rented for 3 silver a month back in Port Moranko.

For now, he was stood in a gigantic wood and goat's leather dome structure, flanked by Obasi and Jaheem. Their version of town hall, he guessed. Space for a couple of hundred people to sit, and with a ceiling not even the prince had a hope of bumping his head on.

In front of him was a wooden throne. The thickness of its base elevated it a good couple of feet; the seat and its back were clothed in what looked like lion skin, while the arms were draped with unmistakable spots of leopard leather. To either side were rows of spacious—albeit less grandiose—sitting places at ground level, on which were folded blankets of smaller furs sewn together. Looked like fox and rabbit blends. Fancy. Fumes of burning incense rose from the hewn centre of a rock plinth in the far corner, filling the air with woody, earthy puffs. Smelled a lot better than the cow-shit and stale tobacco at O' Malley's. In the distance, excited shrieks and chattering of small children playing were punctuated by occasional musings from goats and sheep made public.

And in came the boss man. Booker took off his beaver felt safari hat as a show of respect, holding it by the weathered brim. The king was tall at a few inches above Booker, and broad shouldered like his son. He eased into the throne, resting his meaty forearms on the trophies from predators laid low. A big man, but his movement was slow; the black of his hair faded into grey.

Booker realised the two men at his side were knelt. Headwear removal wasn't enough. Hesitating, he began to bend his knee, but was interrupted by a dismissive wave of hand and one word in Yakanaka language which caused Obasi and Jaheem to return to standing.

"Let us dispense with the formalities, Mr Shaw. You know who I am; I know you are. Suffice to say I am incredibly happy you are here to rid us of this demon," said the king with a wheeze that betrayed breathing problems. His manner was direct but not rude; the tone he used soft. "I will assemble a hunting party of our 50 finest braves to accompany you, led by my son Jaheem."

"That is mighty kind of you, King Zuberi, but I—"

Yakanaka language was chirped from the dome's entrance. He turned to see who had entered.

Holy Christmas! A tribal beauty was brightening the tent more than any torch could. She was radiant in a matching bodice and short skirt of beads coloured in bright yellow, blue and pink; the outfit having a sizeable gap which showed all contours on her svelte abdomen. Around 5'7, her slender sculpted limbs were a perfect combination of athleticism and femininity. And man, the sugar bumps. Goddamn beads. Why couldn't she follow her prince's example?

Giving a brief bow, she sauntered to the king's hand and kissed and pressed her forehead against it; speaking in sweet bubbling lilts—of which he understood nothing—she then curled next to the throne. Covering with the slinky fur blanket, only her shoulders, arms and feet were left exposed. Elegant toes—the nails painted in alternate red and white—peeked out, dangling; they curled and rubbed against each other. Shiny long braids hung in effortless glory as she tilted her head and looked at Booker.

He heard Jaheem give a soft grunt of disapproval. The king outstretched his palm towards the girl, saying, "My daughter, Tinotenda"—he turned to face her with a look of unconvincing rebuke—"who I told not to attend this meeting."

Language changing to English; the tone remained melodious, as she replied with a pout, "Sorry father. I had to welcome the great hunter. Forgive me."

King Zuberi sighed. A relenting smile spread on his tired face. "Well, go on then. Hurry up."

Her bunny rabbit brown eyes looked straight into his; the eyelids shadowed in aqua blue. Full lips parting to form something between smirk and smile, she said, "Welcome, great hunter."

The husky tone made his ears tingle. He gave a bow at the waist, replying, "Thank you, erm, princess."

Zuberi wagged a finger. "Now be quiet. Only the men will speak. Do not make your father angry." The chiding was mild; spoken in English for Booker's benefit.

She pulled the furs higher, exposing her feet further. Beads let out tiny wooden whispers as they shifted and rubbed together.

Wrinkling her painted toes again, she stared straight at Booker and purred, "Yes, father."

"You were, saying, Mr Shaw?"

He could feel sweat dripping down his abdomen; the buttons nearest his neck were growing constrictive. Aware the young lady was still gawking at him, he had to do an internal brain shake. 500 silver. Focus your eyes on the king offering you 500 silver.

"Ah, yes, King Zuberi, as I was saying, that is mighty kind of you to offer an escort of braves, but I do find more people mean more noise, more potential casualties, more supplies to carry, and so on. In my experience, it's best to travel light and in a small party. May I suggest Prince Jaheem and Obasi accompany to provide advice and assistance as necessary?"

The king mulled for a moment, then gave a thoughtful nod. "As you wish. How soon can you begin?"

"The day after tomorrow. I'll need one day to clean my equipment, check everything's working properly, discuss the terrain with Prince Jaheem and Obasi and think about a plan of action. Is there a place nearby where I can safely discharge a few shots?"

"Yes, we have a ground for archery. It is up the path across from your tent."

"That is fantastic. If you could kindly inform everyone not to go near the archery area until after noon, I would appreciate it. No doubt people would be curious to see me fire my guns, and I find crowds a distraction."

In the corner of his eye, he thought he saw the girl stifle a chuckle behind the fluffy edge of her fur covering. Had he said something funny?

"Fine." The king rasped at Jaheem and Obasi. They nodded and began talking among themselves.

He thanked the king and excused himself. Still thinking about that beauty when he lay in his cowhide hammock, he swore to clear his mind of distractions before going anywhere near giant teeth.

Early the next morning, he woke feeling refreshed. The absence of beer meant his sleep hadn't been disturbed by getting up to piss; he decided—in theory—to spend more time away from O' Malley's. But then decisions like that were easy when you had no money.

In the opposite corner to his hammock was a high wooden table with a clay jug and a bowl packed with fruit. He glugged, peeled and crunched. The bananas were rich and sweet, the apples zesty and dripping juice with every bite. Obasi was right about the soil.

Unlike most tents he'd been in, this one had a floor of well-swept black slate. And it didn't creak like the boards in his hotel room. The Yakanaka had talented artisans. And he was thankful for that when laying out his arsenal. Nothing worse than trying to clean and oil weapons on a mucky floor.

One hour later, he'd finished maintenance and was ready to take them for live fire. Hanging the straps of their leather scabbards over his bulging shoulders, he stepped into the village's empty streets. He breathed cool air and strode up a winding incline towards the practice area; sunrise had not long passed, and the sky was still opening its eyelids.

The village pathways were paved with slate—same type as the tent floor—and their edges lined with large, smooth stones. They were painted white, which he assumed was to make them easier to see in poor light. Impressive. Parallel with the paths were lush grass embankments crowned with bushes of flowers and berries; their dew-sprinkled colours of purple, pink and orange glistening in the sun's waking glow. They stretched in every direction throughout the settlement, which was encircled in a sturdy-looking wooden palisade of shorn tree trunks; their tops carved into spikes and tall enough to keep out roaming predators. Even leaping leopards. Smaller settlements he'd walked through on the island weren't as grandiose, but they still gave the impression of attention paid to order, cleanliness and defence. The people—despite their island's recent suffering—looked healthy, strong and well-fed.

Zuberi was no ordinary tribal king. Aside from being humble and approachable, he'd spent the effort to learn English—when he could have had others translate—and his organisational skills were superb. Walking up the hill with no mud or cow dung caking under his shiny boots, he understood why the British were not welcome on Yakanaka. They tended to ruin beautiful places.

Reaching the crest of the hill, he was met with a spectacular view. And not the mountains, trees or lake beyond the palisade; they were nice enough, but nature's true beauty was concentrated in one small vicinity. Princess Tinotenda was practicing archery.

She was about 20 feet from him down the gentle slope which led to a slate rectangle with low wooden plinths spaced out along its edge. A quiver—fat with red-feathered arrows—lay on the nearest one to the entrance where he stood. Today's outfit was even skimpier than the night before. He approved.

She hadn't seen, so he took a moment to indulge. Her back was towards him as she stretched the bow to full extent. The entire rear of her upper body was bare except for clasps around her slender neck and waist. Muscles flexed in sync with bowstring. A loose cowhide skirt barely concealed her full, round derriere. Lithe calves—which tensed in sharp definition as she aimed—were crisscrossed with leather straps tied in tidy knots under her knees; the material fastening elegant sandals to pretty feet.

The shot was loosed, and it whizzed towards the circular straw target, landing with a faint twanging thud. He walked toward her, trying to keep his eyes off her behind. "Just inside bullseye. Not bad. Not bad at all, princess."

Relaxing her bow arm, she turned and smiled, saying, "Ah, the fearless hunter. Good morning." The bodice matched her skirt in style and sensuality. Tight against plump breasts, large nipples poked into its material. Girl was blessed.

The thick soles of his military boots saw him standing 6'4, dwarfing her. He put hands on hips as three heavy guns dangled from his powerful frame. Blonde locks swaying in gentle breeze, he replied, "Good morning, princess. Although you're only half right."

Tilting her head, she asked, "I don't understand?"

"About the fearless hunter. I am indeed a hunter, but the so-called fearless ones tend to meet their end between teeth," he said, working his green eyes. "Good to keep a little fear, in case you have to run real fast."

Giggling, she leaned on the longbow, replying, "You're funny. Although I don't think any Yakanaka man would agree with you."

"Well, your father did bring me here because I do things differently, I guess."

Her smile melting to solemn, she nodded and said, "Yes, he did, and we are very happy to have you here. Thank you for helping us, Mr Shaw."

"Call me Booker."

"Call me Tinotenda."

"Ok, Tinotenda. And I do recall"—he clunked his rifles across one of the low tables— "requesting from your father that I be left alone here this morning."

Her face brightened. "Oops," she said with a mischievous smirk.

He didn't tend to get angry at ladies, royalty or not. "Yea, yea, oops indeed." They laughed. "I guess being the king's daughter makes you confident you won't get in trouble, eh?"

She scoffed at his question. "My father has lots of wives and lots of daughters. But they do as they're told. I push my luck as much as possible. Like now. May I watch you fire your weapons?"

"Isn't that why you came here?" he asked as he slid the 12-gauge pump action shotgun from its scabbard, and tipped it back with one hand to rest the barrel on his shoulder, swaggering.

"That's a yes. Ok go ahead."

"Hmm. Doesn't look like I have a choice then? Ok, take at least ten steps back please. And put your fingers in your ears like this"—he gestured with his free index— "cause the 12-gauge gives out a fair shout."

She ambled a half dozen steps, but kept her arms folded. "I want to hear the noise."

Holding the shotgun tight against his shoulder and aiming downrange, he braced and said from the side of his mouth, "Ok, if you insist."

Bang! The gun thundered a deer slug across the field in a smoky cloud of sulphur. Booker—who'd grown tolerant of harsh sound—looked across to see her standing with hands over ears; the button nose wrinkled. "It's so loud," she said, wafting the sour fumes away as they blew towards her.

Continuing to watch—but now following his instructions—she stood further back as he tested the 12-gauge's loading and ejection system with more shots, then moved to the 44 calibre long scope under action, and finally the elephant gun. He didn't see it—due to being focused on the target—but he knew that double-barrelled boomstick's bellow made her jump. The hefty 4-gauge shells had 3 times more black powder than deer slugs. One well-placed shot was always enough, no matter the quarry.

"That was great! And what about those?" she asked, pointing to the shiny-handled revolvers strapped on his chest.

"Oh, I eh, tested both recently. I think I'll save the bullets."

She stepped close to him, her chest pushed proud and mouth pouty. "May I fire one? They look so beautiful."

Struggling to keep his gaze above her chin, he replied "Well, I'm not so sure about that. 45 has quite a kick for a little lady. Don't want you whacking yourself in the head with it. No offence, intended."

Grinning, she said, "No problem. You can help me."

"Well, still not sure."

"But I am." She stepped in front of him, facing the target. "Come closer. I want to fire a pistol."

He hesitated. "Hmm I'd have to touch you to help out. Not

sure about that. Your husband would take issue…"

Twisting round, she hooked two slender fingers into the thick strap of his shoulder holster and tugged. "I don't have a husband."

"Oh. Well, then Jaheem."—he turned to look at the entrance — "I don't think he'd take too kindly to me touching his little sister."

She tutted. "He is still in bed getting spoiled by his wives. Now, tell me, are women in Kentucky made of glass?"

The question threw him. "Uh…no."

"Good. Neither am I. Now come closer. I won't break." Little bossy boots. Which in a funny way he liked.

"Ok, one shot, but that's it."

He moved forwards; she backwards. Her bare back rubbed his shirt. The pert leather-clad behind he'd admired was now pressed tight against his crotch. Cinnamon and vanilla bean scents were doing exotic dances up his nose. Silky braids scratched stubble. What the hell, he rested his chin on top of her head. She eased even further back against his body. To his silent delight.

Sliding a chunky revolver from its holster, he said, "Ok, but you do exactly as I say"—he held the gun outstretched and pointed to the trigger with his sinewy biceps pressing against her — "and don't touch this here until I say, ok?"

"Yes, sir." Damn, that was a kitten's meow. He hoped the trip to Yakanaka wouldn't end with ten banana fingers choking him to death.

He placed the handle into her palms, and she tightened them around the hard ivory and gleaming chrome. Arms parallel as he steadied and instructed, pink pressed against onyx. The skin was so smooth. Now fully awoken, the sun bathed their huddled bodies in its rays. And it wasn't the only thing risen from slumber.

Crack! A gust of smoke billowed. He was impressed by how she managed the recoil with only a slight flinch. But then she began cocking the hammer for a second shot. "Hey little—"

"Are you not enjoying teaching me?" she asked, wriggling

against him.

He didn't want to end the embrace. "Do you normally hug men you've just met, Tiny Tender?"

Booker got butted in his crotch with, well, her butt—which wasn't the worst thing he'd ever been struck with—as she asserted, "I am not hugging; I am learning to use a new weapon."

The next five shots were an odd experience for him: cosy gunfire.

∞∞∞

This was no good. Pointing to a map of Yakanaka, Obasi was detailing: the coastal terrain, the croc's territory, locations where frequent attacks had happened, surrounding villages, and where they would base. Vital stuff. And all he could think of was Tinotenda.

After emptying the 45's cylinder, she'd bid him good day and slinked up the hill, her majestic hips waving goodbye. He'd struggled to conceal his excitement on the walk back. So much for no distractions. At least she wouldn't be on the hunt; he'd be able to immerse himself in the tracking, baiting and scanning necessary to take down the beast. His mind would clear once he was at work amongst men.

Jaheem lifted back the tent's flap, stooped and entered. "I have been talking to my father. My sister will join us on the hunt."

So much for that plan. "Ok...and why is that?"

"She wants to see the beast that killed our mother die. As vengeance. It is not ideal, but I cannot deny her that right."

"Well, maybe I could talk to King Zuberi ab—"

"And neither can our father. It is the Law of the Sun, Mr Shaw. Do not worry about Tinotenda. She is strong and fast. If the demon comes close, she can run. There is no shame in it for a woman." said Jaheem with a firm smile and nod as if to say the matter was closed for discussion.

500 silver. Avoiding teeth. Those were what to focus on.

∞∞∞

"Cleansing ritual?" Booker asked, over heavy slap and splash.

"Yes. Before hunting or battle, our braves bathe here, to let the sacred water wash away any hidden fear," replied Tinotenda.

He stared at the waterfall. Surrounded by steep cliff face, water gushed from the central edge in a frothy white flow, battering onto the rock pool's shimmering surface. There was a grassy embankment shaded with trees next to the path where they'd entered. She was sat on it cross-legged and picking little white and yellow flowers from between green blades, beside a pile of leather packs and weapons.

And the two tribesmen's clothes. They were already swimming and bathing in the pool, naked. With everyone geared up and ready to trek, he'd expected to be led out one of the gates. Instead they'd stayed within the palisade encirclement and followed the big man up a steep hill. Before he'd stripped and stepped into the water, Jaheem had suggested that all braves—regardless of their origins—should take part in the cleansing ritual.

"So"—she gestured up and down his body with the tips of her palms— "undress. You can leave your clothes beside me. I won't steal them," she said with a bite of her lower lip.

"Just take off all my clothes, here in public, right in front of a lady?"

"Yes," she replied with a tut, as if he'd asked a silly question. The mouth wasn't betraying pleasure in his situation, but her eyes were telling a different tale.

"And you're just going to sit here and watch me? You don't have to cleanse too?" If he was going to give a show, he preferred to receive one in return.

"Only men are considered as braves. A woman cannot do the ritual. And women in Yakanaka only reveal themselves to their husbands."

"Well, ain't that a fine double standard if I ever heard it."

"Welcome to Yakanaka," she said with a playful laugh. "Now don't be shy. Get undressed. I won't look...much." The last word was whispered under her breath, barely audible as she began picking another tiny flower.

He made a visor from his hand and peered across the embankment and pool to see Obasi and Jaheem standing chest and waist deep respectively in the same level of water, waving him over, to take part. Giving the thumbs up, he shouted an "ok", and they returned to horseplay, with Jaheem picking up Obasi in a bear hug then throwing him half a dozen feet to land with a whoosh of white spray. Seemed more like a bath for big kids than a sacred ceremony.

"Fine, if that's what's expected, guess I'd better obey the rules." He started unbuttoning his shirt with confident plucks.

"You honour us. Thank you," she said with a sincere smile, which had reformed to a thin smirk by the time his undergarments were folded on top of his clothes.

Naked as nature, he stepped into the pool, sensing eyes on his behind. Knee deep in chilly water and feeling smooth stone rub his feet, he turned to face her. She was pretending to pick flowers.

Taking a glance at himself, he knew there was nothing to be ashamed of; he was lean, conditioned and all man. Bouts of drinking and card playing between contracts hadn't made the muscles on his abdomen succumb to belly fat. Mostly because he ended up frittering all his money away and having nothing to eat. Kept a fella trim. And lifestyle habits—good or bad—made no difference to old faithful, hanging between his legs. Yep, this was a rare treat for a lady to lay eyes on.

Tinotenda looked up and stared at him. Hands on hips, he was exposed. Enjoy, little princess.

She placed a dainty palm across her mouth, laughing.

"Something funny?" he asked with raised voice, feeling a poke at his pride.

Removing her hand, she leaned forward, scrutinising his naked body from knee to neck. "How long have you been in Africa? Your body is like milk."

"5 years. Something wrong with milk?"

Rolling her eyes, she replied, "It's interesting. I've never seen a white man before"—she motioned in blunt fashion at his crotch — "and the hair around your manhood is blonde. It's so different. But anyway, I do like milk…"

"You do, do you?" He was strutting.

After staring at the long thick cock hanging between his legs, she met his eyes. "Oh, Booker. You have a big one."

"Excuse me?" The opinion wasn't surprising but the blunt delivery of it was. Especially from a princess.

"A big ego. Is that how you say it? 'Ee-go'?" She drank in the view, unable to hide a huge smile. Brilliant teeth sparkled in the bright sunlight. He laughed and swam across to the others. What a little bit of mischief.

With the cleansing ritual done, the men dressed and off they all headed towards West Yakanaka. The journey had begun.

∞∞∞

Jaheem and Obasi had insisted on carrying the long guns—along with their own spears and bows—which left him walking in relative comfort. His backpack was a fair weight, but nothing taxing. The safari hat's brim was doing an excellent job as he scanned across the sun-soaked plains on either side of the worn-grass path they strode along. On the far horizon to the left, the lake's placid surface sparkled under rays like polished crystal. On the right, a broad plateau of lush fields, trees and streams stretched to steep mountains.

Travelling in close formation and with a 6 hour walk to the village of Budiriro, he saw a good opportunity to reinforce crocodile hunting principles discussed the day before.

"So, gentlemen"—he turned to Tinotenda and tipped his hat — "and lady. Since we have plenty time before we reach our destination, I thought we might discuss one or two things to keep us all safe."

To the leathery rustle and bump of packs, quivers and scabbards shifting on shoulders, he reminded his companions of key information. "First and foremost, I will oversee this hunt. I know this is your country and I'm mindful of your status, but King Zuberi didn't hire me for my good looks and charm"—he saw her stifle a giggle— "so, please follow my instructions and we'll put an end to this problem and all come back breathing with arms and legs attached. That clear?"

Nodding grunts came from the men; a resonant "yes" was declared by the beauty. She was wearing a modest knee-length dress of cow suede, topped with a bodice of black and white beads draped to her midriff. No eyeshadow, pretty paint on toenails or tantalizing scents of spice. He was grateful.

"Ok, good. Important: We hunt in daytime only. By the time sunset hits, I want us far from the water. Crocs can be hard enough to spot in the light. Doesn't make any sense to go looking for them in the dark. Everyone clear?"

Same response from all. Good. He pointed to the fields of tall emerald crops passing by on their right. "That is the kind of terrain I want to avoid walking in, whether day or night." He came to a halt, stooped and swiped an imaginary line across his boot at ankle level. "Anything above that height we will try not to walk in, taking detours if necessary. You don't want to be wandering in thick grass and step into a pair of jaws. Is everyone clear on that? Please do say if I'm talking too fast, or if my Kentucky accent is muddling the—"

"What's a 'detour'?" asked Tinotenda as the party began descent between embankments peppered with clumps of bright yellow flowers.

"It means to take an alternative path to the one originally intended."

"Oh, ok," she said, taking a—deliberate—stumble and

steadying herself on his forearm with a lingering grasp. Smooth skin again. "Oops, sorry. Like that?" She was good at displaying feigned innocence.

Focus. "Furthermore, do not go near the water's edge unless I say so. And even more importantly, do not go in the water at any point. Even if you think it's too shallow for a croc to hide in. They are sneaky creatures, folks. Let's stay alert and stay alive. Y'all clear?"

Their trek continued with Booker laying down further rules as they occurred to him. Passing through villages and scattered farmsteads, they were gifted goatskins swollen with water, chunky banana bunches and loaves of soft steamed bread; little girls flocked round Tinotenda and clung to her skirts, holding up chubby digits in hopes of being lifted and hugged. She was rarely without one cradled in each arm, smothering them in kisses; the older girls—not yet women—hung on her side, sharing whispers between shy glances at Booker. Tips of his hat saw giggles burst into guffaws. The boys walked with excitement and pride alongside himself and the two tribesmen, gathering in ecstatic huddles, pointing at his pistols, clapping, whooping and chanting songs.

This was the Africa he loved. Nothing like the sludge and squalor of Port Moranko.

∞∞∞

"Aren't they beautiful?" asked Tinotenda. "So strong but so gentle." Wary of the branches' sharp thorns, she snapped another twiglet from the acacia tree and pushed it towards the giraffe's mouth. Its darting tongue twisted around the rich leaves and gobbled the offering.

They were—according to Obasi—around 1 hour from Budiriro with daylight left, so had decided to seek temporary refuge in shade. Continuous walking in hot sun had sapped Booker's energy; khaki shirt now one shade darker, it stuck to him. His pistol holsters were damp, as was the inside of his hat. He took it off, brushed aside soaked locks and fanned himself with the wide brim. No breeze to supply respite, just distant cluck and chatter of birds.

He and Tinotenda were stood at the edge of a cliff face, beside which were the tops of an acacia thicket. As the group had rested on the grass guzzling water, a giraffe's long-chinned head had appeared from a break in the branches. The tribesmen's interest had lasted two minutes before they returned to reclining and swigging at their waterskins. A quip was made about finally meeting someone taller than the prince, which resulted in Obasi getting a generous slosh over his shiny cranium.

She had continued to feed and pet the lanky guest, her mood joyous. He was snapping off twigs and passing them along. He liked seeing her smile. They were just out of earshot, but noise from the giraffe's slimy slurps reminded him to watch his own tongue.

"Well, certainly wouldn't try and feed some other animals this way. So, yea, gentle I guess"—he reached between the thorns to pluck another leafy morsel— "but I did see one of these kick a lioness to death one time. Was a hell of a stomp. Lion's head damn near came off."

She rubbed the giraffe's bony snout, giggling as it snatched and munched. "Defending its babies, of course. Any mother would do the same. They only fight when forced to. It should be the same with people."

Running her eyes over his swollen biceps and burly chest, she gestured to the pistols. Her voice was soft, solemn. "Some monsters must die. But you don't like killing...do you?"

Wiping his dripping brow, he replied, "Nope. Matter of fact I don't. Been getting mighty tired of it, truth be told. Seem to spend half my life waiting for someone to offer me money for killing something, then the other half killing myself with the proceeds."

"Then why live that way? You are a man; you can do what

you like. Choose another path."

"It ain't no way to live, that's for sure. Especially at 35 years old. Maybe I'll take the silver and buy myself a boat trip back to Kentucky. Could be a cattle drover or a cow hand. I'd rather work with animals than kill them."

She took a discreet glance in the direction of her brother. He and Obasi were laid back with packs like pillows, bickering over some—no doubt—triviality. "Do you like Africa? Would you stay if you had a… different life here?" The volume of her voice was reducing. He copied.

"I love Africa. And honestly, I love Yakanaka."

The answer agitated her. A slight frown spread across her beautiful features. Had he said something wrong?

"Do you like…Yakanaka women?" she asked in a hushed tone, continuing to take twiglets but with face towards the giraffe as it caught the snacks and sucked them in.

He took a sideways look at Jaheem. "You mean even the ones who tell me to strip naked?" he replied with raised eyebrows.

Lips pursed; air pressure puffed out her cheeks. She put hand over lips to muffle chuckles. Once the brief giggle fit had stopped, he passed her two more bundles of leaves. The giraffe's dark tongue was outstretched, licking at her hand, trying to wrap round the greenery with slick, hungry slaps. They laughed at the animal's comical determination.

A butterfly floated onto her exposed shoulder; the striking sky blue and scarlet pattern of its delicate wings causing her surprise and delight. He took a quiet step back. "Absolutely lovely."

She craned her neck with care, so as not to disturb. "Yes, it is."

"I wasn't talking about the butterfly."

Her face was alight with sparkles of happiness; the confident manner faded into simpers of moist-lipped submission.

"Mr Shaw, perhaps it is time to continue?" called Obasi. He and Jaheem were gearing up, slinging on packs and weapons. The butterfly continued its graceful journey. Time to push on.

She gave the giraffe's broad forehead one last rub with her palm and ruffled its jutting ears, saying, "Strong but gentle. So beautiful."

"You said that already." He gave a cocky smile and wink, putting his safari hat back on.

Turning to walk away she whispered, "I wasn't talking about the giraffe."

∞∞∞

Booker was pleased with Budiriro as a base for expeditions. About 1 mile from the croc's territory and perched atop a hill of short grass, its shoulder-high stone wall was thick and sturdy, with the sole entrance being via solid timber gates. Perfect.

Now he just had to persuade Tinotenda to stay within while the men hunted. Truth be told, he would have rather had all three of his companions do the same so he could work alone. But asking Obasi and Jaheem—proud Yakanaka warriors—to remain in safety would be taken as a grievous insult.

With her being a woman, he might be able to swing it. She didn't need to see the beast die in front of her. Once he'd shot it, Jaheem could cut the tip off its tail—or a foot—and bring it to her as a blood-soaked trophy. It wasn't like she was going to be able to kill the damn thing herself anyway. He'd make her see reason; it was better than risking her getting hurt.

They'd arrived in the late afternoon and he'd climbed into a hammock after peeling off sticky clothes and moist boots. A welcome slumber enveloped soon after. Upon waking, he checked his brass pocket watch—the device needing an expert clean—to see he'd been out for two hours. Orange hues seeping under the tent's edges told him it was dusk. Not bad. Meant he would still sleep later in the night and be up at dawn for the first day of tracking.

There was a large wooden jug, basin and folded cloth beside

his cot. Bending his head into the basin, he poured water over dank blonde locks. The liquid massaged his scalp and neck with revitalising shivers. He wet the cloth, washed and then dressed. Putting on a clean undershirt under his suspenders, he decided against a shirt or pistols. The air felt cool and he wanted maximum exposure against his skin after the sweltering trek. Fishing through equipment, he found his British military bayonet in its boiled leather sheath and slid it inside his right boot. Weapons made him feel secure, despite the dislike he held for them.

Budiriro was smaller than the capital—which he had now learned was named Kumhara Kwamambo—but the order and cleanliness hadn't diminished. People were just as friendly too. Strolling along the main torch-lit path, he met waves, grins, greetings—in English and Yakanaka—and shouted tributes. From further up the hill, he could hear persistent heavy thumps on drum leather; the low-pitched tones filling the amber sky as sunlight bid the world goodnight. He wondered what the music was for.

A timid little girl raced in front of him to offer a massive banana and say simply, "For you" before scampering away. He turned to see her huddling proud parents; their sheepish smiles saying they'd been shy about approaching. "Thank you. Thank you so much. Mighty kind of you," he said while peeling back the skin. Size was huge. Reminded him of Jaheem's pecker at the waterfall. He discarded that thought to enjoy the fruit without prejudice while he walked further into the village's heart.

And talking of the prince; there he was. Sat in a central square of grass, surrounded by doting men, including the ever present Obasi. Booker approached from behind, but their excited chatter betrayed his presence. The watermelon-sized cranium turned and a wide smile broke. "Booker Shaw! Please come. Meet my cousins. And I have something to show you."

After Booker had been introduced to a dozen tribesmen one at a time, the prince pointed to a nearby large tent and gave an order in Yakanaka. Three tribesmen jogged inside before carrying the surprise item across to Jaheem, who grasped it in both hands.

It was the biggest goddamn spear he'd ever seen.

Jaheem stood around 7'2-4, so the top of it being far above his ebony head meant the whole thing was 9 feet plus. The bulbous tip was a peak cut for piercing, with jagged sides designed to tear and slice. Lowered for scrutiny, Booker assessed sharpness with gentle presses. A well-crafted javelin indeed. But only a man Jaheem's size and strength could even wield it, never mind launch the damn thing. He was given a try of the weighty wood and iron. Felt like about 4 elephant guns combined. Impressive. Except bullets didn't have to be thrown or swung.

"Mighty fine, Jaheem. A gift from your cousins here?"

"Yes, they have suffered the worst from the devil in the lake and want it dead." His tone turned speculative. "They asked me even now if they can accompany the hunt…"

"We'll tell them where to find the carcass," he said with a light pat on Jaheem's bulky arm.

"Yes, of course." The disappointment in his voice was clear.

"What are those drums for?" asked Booker, changing the subject.

"A girl from the village was given in marriage earlier. Now is time for the union. The drums will play until the husband emerges from their tent and requests they stop."

It wasn't an unpleasant sound, but he didn't understand why a newly married couple had to get down to business with loud musical accompaniment. In his experience, not all traditions made sense, so he decided to leave it. "Ok, tomorrow we'll head off 1 hour after dawn to ensure we have proper light. Can y'all meet me beside the front gate? Make sure you've got plenty water and provisions, as it's gonna be a long day."

He saw Tinotenda strolling up the hill, accompanied by two young girls. Perfect. Now was time for that talk.

∞∞∞

"Mind if I join you, ladies?" He stood in front of Tinotenda and her teenage companions. They lay on plump couches fashioned from wood, straw and goat leather, overlooking tents spread across the hill's broad and gnarled grass terrain. The drums were still going. Two large sets sat on either side of the tent's entrance where—he assumed—the bride and groom were getting real cosy. He was surprised to see the large cylindrical instruments being thumped by women, not men. Their arms were ropey. He guessed they'd had practice.

"This is the women's corner. Men are not supposed to sit here," she said in factual manner. One of the girls whispered in her ear, causing a tight-lipped smile to raise her delicate cheekbones higher.

"Oh I—"

"But my cousins and I want you to stay, and you are an honoured guest in the village. I don't think it will be a problem."

He perched on one of the couches facing the group, feeling the frame creak. Designed with women's weight in mind. "Thank you. So, I—"

The other girl now budged close to Tinotenda, whispering with hands cupped. She could have shouted out loud for all the Yakanaka language he knew.

"Has anyone ever told you its rude to whisper, young lady?" he asked with a kindly frown. This resulted in both girls breaking into giggles, their shy eyes averting his, cuddling into their older cousin.

Tinotenda kissed each of them on the forehead and pinched their cheeks. "They say you are handsome."

He sucked air and blew it out in a popped puff. "Well, they ain't blind, I guess. Thank you very much"—he turned to the other girl— "and thank you too. Erm, might I have a private word?"

"My cousins don't understand English except for a few simple words. You can talk freely"—she rubbed their braided heads and spoke in Yakanaka— "I've told them to be quiet. They won't interrupt."

"Ok, fine. So, I—"

"No."

"What? I haven't even—"

"No, I'm not staying here while you hunt the monster. It killed my mother. I will see it die," she said with an assertive stare. The two girls snuggled at her sides lay gazing at him. Thudding bellows of base continued to resonate across the now star speckled night sky.

He sighed. Ok, so she was sharp. But he wasn't so easily bossed around. "Has it occurred to you that you might get hurt? Or even killed? I don't want to see that happen."

Breaking into a smile, she said, "You have a very sweet heart. But I'm a woman, not a child. I'm not afraid."

"Thing's killed almost 50 people. You should be afraid. Remember what I said about fearless hunters and teeth?"

She nodded. "I have my brother. Did you see his spear?"

"Pretty hard not to."

"And I have you."

"What?"

"I have you to protect me. You don't want to protect me?"

"Of course, I do. That's exactly—"

"Good, then I will be safe. I won't change my mind. And my father gave me permission. He is king of Yakanaka, not you. Is that clear?"

Wanting to protect her was why he hoped she'd stay put in Budiriro. With a relenting exhalation he said, "Fine, but you do not go near that water and you do as I say. Is *that* clear?"

"Yes, sir." There was that kitten voice again. Half in gentle mockery, half to rile his masculine tendencies, he suspected.

The drums stopped. Sudden absence of their rumbling rhythm caused keen silence.

The groom was handing what looked like silver coins to the drummers. They stood and began carrying off their equipment.

"What's the point of all that?"

"It is to conceal the sound of the bride's pleasure. The wedding night is her first experience of a man. Things often get loud, and the tent skins are thin."

"Oh. Well, what if the happy couple decide to go for round two, later in the night?" he asked with a wry grin.

"It's hoped the woman can control herself better the second time."

"I see. And do you want someone playing drums for you soon?"

"I want but..." Her face was pained, awkward.

"I'm sorry. I didn't mean to cause offence. I forget myself sometimes. I do apologise."

"No, it's ok. I want to be married but I refuse to share. In Yakanaka, the men can have as many wives as they like. No man has only one wife for long. My brother has six and is always on the hunt for number seven. The women in my country accept it. I will not."

"Your brother did say the Christian way of marriage wasn't too popular in your country."

"For me, it's something I admire very much, even though I didn't always agree with the missionaries' ideas. One man, one woman. I find it beautiful. Don't you think so?"

Being married to six women sounded like a headache. One might be manageable though. "Certainly, seems the preferable choice, I agree."

A look of admiration appeared. "My father is pleading with me to marry. I know I shame him, being unmarried at 25 years, but I will not share. If I marry a man, I am his and he is mine. Nobody else. It's simple."

"Sounds mighty nice, especially when you say it."

Her gaze aimed into his eyes, those beautiful browns smouldering. "Yes. Mighty nice."

∞∞∞

Booker had yet again proven himself the best damn tracker and baiter in Africa. But this time was different. Finding his prize was going to be the end of him.

On his side, dragging himself up saturated sand, with shirt torn and blood-stained, he threw his empty pistols at the abomination advancing with gaping mouth. Their hammers had slammed in rapid percussion until billows of smoke cleared to the sound of redundant clicks and crocodile hiss. Twelve hasty bullets fired at its gargantuan head and neck had delayed the assault. But it was still coming. Bloodied, leaking, but not retreating. The pierce of its pitiless eyes asserting he was the prey, not it.

His futile escape crawl was ended by a smooth rock shelf. Not steep, but too high for him to navigate in time—with his current injuries—before the beast would clamp. It was now upon him; the jaws a jagged cemetery screaming of graves in abundance. Drawing the bayonet from his boot and grasping with the blade pointed down, his mouth was caked in sand and salty blood as he braced, screaming, "I'm gonna cut your fuckin' eyes out!"

The day had started in a far more optimistic manner. It was the second morning of hunting when the sky's shine had highlighted a compression in thin grass. The width of whatever had been slithering around was cause for concern. He'd readied the elephant gun, winding its leather strap tight around his supporting arm and keeping it close into his shoulder. Following the track led them down a mild incline to a stretch of beach about thirty feet wide, flanked on either side by high ridges. The sandy slope gave easy access to and from the lakeside, and a spacious trench between rock shelves meant any croc could ascend and descend without obstacle. A beautiful spot, but he got the feeling an ugly presence had taken to malingering in it.

The small ridge with the best position for taking a shot into the cove had enough space for him and his equipment, and no more. That suited him. He didn't want any excited companions stepping in front of a barrel at the last second or cluttering elbow manoeuvrability when precise aiming was called for. The ridge on the other side was broader and—more importantly—higher than the one he'd chosen. He wanted risk to his fellow hunters to be minimal, especially the lovely Tinotenda. Assigning them to the high spot, he made the excuse that more space would be suitable for drawing bows and throwing Jaheem's spear if the chance arose. The reality was Booker knew the hunt would end in smoke and lead. Still, he was impressed by how nimbly Obasi and Tinotenda scaled the steep 20-foot slope. Jaheem clambered up within three grunting heaves: agile for such a big man.

 He unpacked bait from a leather bundle. It was a lamb cut into five pieces. After shaking out blood and innards onto the surrounding sand, he placed the chunks in a heap about halfway up the beach. Most hunters he'd met thought crocs smelled food best when it was underwater. He didn't agree. Experience had shown baiting on land drew them faster, usually without fail. Obasi had assured there were no lions or leopards known to prowl in the immediate region. If the scent did cause any cats to show up, they'd be having lamb surprise. More blood in the air to tempt the lake's beast towards swift reckoning.

 Clasping the elephant gun's sturdy oak stock and resting it over his forearm, he kneeled, leaned against the rock and scanned the shimmering surface. Could be a long wait. Miniscule wisps of soft lamb's wool were stuck to his palms with sticky tinges of blood. Smell was fresh, metallic. If that croc was anywhere nearby, it'd be unlikely to resist the meat's tantalising odours.

 Clouds started to smother the sun; their white puffs mottled grey. Drizzle drifted across the cove, brought by a breeze which strengthened into moderate gusts. Small ripples became waves; their tops curling and crashing on the beach in frothy cascades. He wiped moisture from his rifle with a cloth and continued to scrutinise the choppy expanse, which had turned several shades darker.

 Tinotenda was knelt. Vigilant, her bow remained in hand, an arrow knocked. She looked across occasionally to give a thumbs up, which he returned. God, so beautiful. He wanted to smile but held off. Plenty time for that later. The two men were sat leaning against the side of the wide ledge. Jaheem's enormous feet dangling at the edge; the tree trunk spear nearby.

After a couple of hours, a wave of notable size started to surge toward shore. Unable to see for driving spray, he squinted with palm cupped on eyebrows. Its flow was rapid, as if more than wind was powering its pulse. As it neared, he saw the swelling surf had a scaly top. And teeth. Huge ones.

As it came skulking from the water, he was mesmerised and aghast at the croc's bloated size. Its colossal head began devouring the lamb, crunching and cracking, while a gigantic body tapered to a spiked tail snaking far back into the lake. Damn thing must have been 27-28 feet long. Leviathan lifted from Biblical lore.

A barrage of hatred-filled screams and arrows erupted from his companions. Jaheem was aiming his spear, jostling for position while trying not to barge anyone with it. Damn stupid size of a weapon. Tinotenda and Obasi were swift in their knocks and shots, the arrows—his fletched in white, hers red—jabbed into armoured skin only to be shaken loose like toothpicks as it hissed in rage at the unexpected welcome.

He braced the elephant gun tight against his shoulder. He wanted to aim but was disturbed by Tinotenda's reckless determination. Angling to get a more exact strike, her sandal-clad foot stretched further down the slope's smoother area, which was gleaming from myriad spits of drizzle. She slipped and began a careering slide towards the croc's merciless jaws.

"Jesus fucking Christ! No!"

With her feet inches from the monster's lunges, the meaty hand of Jaheem clamped on her wrist, hauling to safety with Herculean strength. Thank God! But she was soon knocking another arrow, aiming at the beast again. Goddammit. Booker screamed with the fury only felt towards those beloved. "Stop shooting now! Stand the fuck back! You're gonna get yourself fuckin' killed!"

He was going to end it quick. And then give that woman one fuckin' hell of a scolding, royalty or not. But agitation proved distracting. It meant when shifting footing to aim the 4-gauge cannon, he placed his boot on a small section of the ridge which was weak, cracked. It crumbled. Combined with the rifle's weight distributed on the same side, balance was lost. His hat tumbled and he soon followed, bouncing over 12 feet of pointed rock, battering the ribs and shoulder on his right side. He landed face first in compacted sand with a wallop. The elephant gun clattered onto the beach a few feet from the rampaging crocodile.

That was when he'd drawn and unleashed with his revolvers. Struggling to breathe, dazed; half the damn bullets probably missed.

And this was where he found himself now. Kissing the Reaper's scythe. Kicking, screaming, the bayonet blade gleaming; the croc's breath was putrid, like vomit and rotten meat. This was it. Here come the teeth!

An arrow landed with fleshy thud, right in the bastard's eye. Spasming, thrashing, its hiss a dozen cobras clashing; it writhed, reared, trying to shake loose the red-feathered wood. The gnarled head swinging like a sledgehammer of tooth and bone; Booker lay flat, his hands up in defence, continuing to clutch the bayonet.

And then a titanic battle scream echoed throughout the cove; followed by Jaheem's spear slamming into the monster's side. The sound was like a heavy boot plunging into thick mud. Waves of sand were being churned, thrown into Booker's face from the beast's flailing. He coughed and spat, grit and tears mingled, but he still made out crimson gushing from its punctured side as Jaheem twisted the spear, wrenching it, crying out to the sun for strength.

The strike had to be fatal; the question was if the croc had enough left in its tank to take a final victim before its demise. A desperate thrash of its hefty skull saw Jaheem side swiped and knocked across the sand onto his knees, reeling. It limped towards him, dying but not dead.

Booker struggled to his feet in sickening pain. He teetered towards the elephant gun, dropping the bayonet and wiping his eyes. Vision stinging, he could barely see the metallic sheen of its barrel. Bending to snatch it, he tied the strap tight and clamped his sand-covered hands onto the fore stock and triggers. Stumbling forward, he drew the gun in to his injured side. Every action agony.

Pointing at the middle of its blurred head, he pulled both triggers at once, releasing a thunderous discharge. The recoil was like a zebra's kick into his fragile bones. His body unable to accept the escalating intensity of pain, he passed out.

∞∞∞

"Mr Shaw"—Tinotenda tugged the tent's entrance flap back to its hanging position after entering— "How was your sleep? Refreshing?"

He was lying on his back in a large cot of cotton pillows and silky furs. The injuries from a week before still smarted but he was recovering with remarkable speed. The luxury tent in Kumhara Kwamambo was a comfortable place to mend.

"Very much so, Mrs Shaw."

She raised an eyebrow. "Well, my father agreed to your request, but remember, we are not yet man and wife. As I told you before, that cannot happen until we've joined our bodies. And your battle wounds have meant the union hasn't been possible, so"—she sauntered past a rack of small spears, running her fingertip across their shafts— "no. I'm afraid we're not married yet."

King Zuberi had lavished him with praise and two clinking purses holding 500 silver. Booker had accepted the former. And then asked for his daughter. He'd explained about finding something more precious than coin. Tinotenda's agreement had been swift. The king—swayed by her pout and pleading eyes—granted the mighty hunter's wish and said no other foreigner would have been deserving.

She'd visited him daily with the sweetest kindness—and adorable fussiness—but sexual intercourse had been forbidden; to speed recuperation until he could fulfil the union properly. The Yakanaka were an all or nothing type of people. Didn't make any difference. He hadn't been up to it anyway.

"How are you feeling now?"—she swept away the lower furs and placed his bare feet in her lap, rubbing toes and soles— "Any stronger…Mr Shaw?" She spoke the syllables like they swam in syrup.

"Well, I had a visitor earlier today. Your brother, in fact."

"Oh?" she stroked the bridge of his foot, preoccupied.

"Yes."

She waited for further information to follow. It didn't. "And?" she shrugged.

He presented his index finger as a signal to wait. The mellow murmur of gentle drumbeats began. "He helped me arrange these. I said I wanted them starting softly."

Squealing with happiness, she pounced, straddling him. Cheeks, teeth, eyes; her whole face was a united smile.

"Ouch, careful honey. You have to be gentle, ok?"

"So sorry, my darling husband"—her moist lips planted a passionate kiss on his— "I promise I'll be gentle. You will relax, and I will do everything."

"Well, don't want to be lazy, I—"

Her tone sharpened. "You will relax, and I will do everything. I am the boss tonight, understand?" Leaning forward, she rested her leather-clad breasts against his bare chest, pushing her probing tongue into his ear canal. Felt like bliss.

"Yes, ma'am."

"I think"—she brushed his blonde fringe— "I have to eat all of you. I am a hungry lioness. I have waited a long time for my taste of man. I will wait no longer."

Whispers had his scalp tingling. That divine blend of cinnamon and vanilla was back on braids brushing against his face, neck and chest. Relaxing back into the soft pillows he said, "Do as you like, lioness."

The drums were sending gentle melodies into the air. "They will have to pound loud to conceal my roar tonight." She sucked his Adam's apple, licking his neck and chin; abrasion between stubble and tongue causing satisfying rasp.

She was bursting with virgin lust, but mindful of injuries when she climbed off and removed the furs. His rugged body was exposed, but the warm night air was accommodating of nudity.

She stood back from the bed and untied her bodice, revealing large, firm breasts; the shape resembled huge grapes. Nipples puffy, they peaked into soft brown tips. What a healthy wife he had. "You like?"

"Yes, ma'am. Hell, yes."

"Good, because they're yours now. Shall I remove my skirt?"

"If you don't, I'll come over there and rip it off. Would be a shame to damage such fine leather."

The skirt was slipped off to reveal shaven sex. Smooth, tight; it had his loins lurching.

"I have never revealed my womanhood to a man before. I hope it pleases you." She licked the tip of her index finger and ran it up and down the slit.

Breathing hard, he said, "Your body's perfect. Turn around."

Her eyelids lowering along with her voice, she nodded. "Oh, I know your favourite part."

Turning, she stood straight, hands by sides. Submitting to inspection. Her behind—like the rest—was carved from ebony tree, athletic, the cheeks full and plump. "You like?"

Appetite was surging. "Come here."

She walked to his side and he took delicate hold of her hand. Then spun her, causing a cheerful yelp of surprise. Putting a firm palm on her stomach, he pulled luscious cheeks close. Kissing soon became licking; frothy bubbles of spit glazed her ample buttocks. He was ravenous. Greedy. He spread her bottom and gorged on secret sweetmeats hidden between folds of royal flesh. It was a banquet. His tongue exploring shameful wonders, she leaned forward and aided, body trembling. Saliva dripped on slate as he slurped and sucked parts tender, pink and puckered.

Drawing air in sharp gasps, moaning, she said, "Darling, I want to do the same but with your manhood."

Kneeling between his spread legs, the feast started without flesh even connecting. Her glinting eyes spoke of gluttony as she inspected his cock and balls. The thick, hard member in palm, she marvelled at veins, rigidity and the contrast of pale and purple between shaft and helmet. "I've never"—she turned the large penis in delicate twists, admiring— "I've never seen a man's snake turn to a spear before. Is it always so…hard? It's like stone."

"Depends on who's handling the spear." Her fingers looked so tiny in contrast to his huge cock.

"Well from now on"—she stopped herself— "Whose spear is this?" Her clasp tightened around his shaft.

"Mi"—he recognized the trick question— "Yours, my darling. Your property."

"Good answer," she said, giving him a squeaking kiss with pressed lips on his cock hat as reward.

She shouted in Yakanaka towards the tent entrance. The drums grew louder. Echoing bass rumbling forth. "Your moans are for my ears only."

Eager lapping bombarded his balls. The sack nibbles were a little too vigorous—as she didn't realise the sensitivity they held—but he enjoyed the mix of pleasure and pain.

Then his cock was celebrated. The hat licked and kissed, she rubbed and pressed it to her chin and cheek, worshipping its masculine vitality, teasing soft blonde hair with tickles of tongue. Sucks started sheepish but become slimy, sloppy; her mouth finishing in pops as she rose for gulps of air before returning to drool and dribble, gobbling and gagging. Arms splayed; Booker was an obedient prisoner of pleasure.

"Are you ready for the union?" she asked, wiping her mouth and positioning to sit.

"God, yes. Please." He was now desperate to enjoy her virgin pussy.

Nestling swollen cock tip between supple lips of sex, she perched, gasping while sliding down his length in delightful, greasy crunches. They were joined in a seat of sexual ecstasy.

His dick was so long and thick it stretched skin to new extents as its pale white shaft jutted out of her lower body. Leaning back with heavy breasts quivering, nipples erect and voice shivering she said, "I am impaled." And once again, head facing the heavens with eyes closed she repeated, "I am impaled."

Gyrating, writhing, wide-eyed in surprise at the delights her own body could bestow, she shocked Booker with a snarled, "I will fuck my fill."

Riding in rhythm with the drums, they grew louder as moans turned to squeals. Screams began releasing from deep inside her; the hammering outside was at a peak as he felt himself unable to hold on. The tight, wet bumps and wriggles of her hips too slick, too taut. Breasts now pressed to his mouth; she commanded, "suck! Suck! Suck!"

Hot, pent-up liquid gushed from their bodies in unison; squirt and flow causing sticky satisfaction as she collapsed forward with exhausted kisses on his panting mouth. He was both empty and full as she dismounted and lay huddled at his side. As her breathing began to slow, she drew tighter, careful not to press his injured ribs. "Is it always so wonderful?"

"I've never experienced anything that incredible before"— he planted a firm kiss on her forehead— "so, I guess we'll make our own special wonders."

Still naked, she poked her head out of the tent flap and paid the drummers. It was against tradition, but then so was their marriage. Before returning to bed, she reached into the pouch of her skirt, and brought out something in her closed hand. "My father had something made for you. A wedding present."

"Really? Well that's mighty kind of him."

"Hold out your hand." She dropped the gift into his palm.

It was a necklace of crocodile teeth. 6 jagged white spikes joined in leather lace.

"Damn, aren't those the ugliest goddamn things you've ever seen?"

"They are. But also, a reminder that good came from evil.

They brought us together."

"Amen to that. And I never want us to be apart."

"Together forever. Let me know when you're ready for round two."

Grateful Thanks

Thank you so much for taking the time to read my work. I hope it brought you some enjoyment.

Sometimes readers are unaware of how important reviews are for authors, particularly new authors such as myself. I would like to respectfully ask that you take a few minutes to leave a review for Bossy on Amazon and/or Goodreads. It will be deeply appreciated.

Best wishes

Florian

Printed in Great Britain
by Amazon